Agnes Mary Frances Robinson

Arden

A Novel: Vol. I

Agnes Mary Frances Robinson

Arden
A Novel: Vol. I

ISBN/EAN: 9783337066819

Printed in Europe, USA, Canada, Australia, Japan

Cover: Foto ©Andreas Hilbeck / pixelio.de

More available books at **www.hansebooks.com**

ARDEN

A NOVEL

BY

A. MARY F. ROBINSON

IN TWO VOLUMES

VOL. I.

LONDON

LONGMANS, GREEN, AND CO.

1883

TO

E. F. POYNTER

IN

FRIENDSHIP AND GRATITUDE

CONTENTS

OF

THE FIRST VOLUME.

ARDEN.

CHAPTER I.

IN THE FOREST OF ARDEN.

THE DAYS are long gone by since under
the trees of Arden fair adventurous dam-
sels wandered in merry outlawry, and
many young gentlemen flocked there
every day to fleet the time carelessly as
in the golden world. No careless gaiety
revels in Arden now; but through the
busy summer hard work for little wage ;
in the winter cold, dreariness, and for the
poor unoccupied privation.

Perhaps those oaks and elms whose
trunks were scored with Orlando's rhymes,

have quite forgotten that their branches
ever sheltered so much youth and gallant
spirit. A few of them are left, gnarled
and decrepit, fenced round with rails,
propped with iron, secured with ropes;
they stand like cumbrous giants among
the younger trees, and support with
difficulty their own extreme old age. At
their feet there is no forest, only miles
of wooded gently undulating fields.

But many of the trees are fallen;
every year with the winds of March their
ranks get thinned and rarer. And all that
is left of Arden is here and there the
name, or the suffix of a name, among the
many villages that sprang up, like mush-
rooms, where the forest first was felled.
Now the villages, too, are old, mossed
over and ruinous.

Not far from Henley in Arden, and
near Wood End, stands a long straggling
village with half-timbered farmhouses and
orchards full of writhen apple-trees; there

are thatched cottages set at intervals beside the lane, and as you walk along the
road you smell the gillyflowers and lilac
long before the flowers, hedged in with
privet, are to be seen themselves ; and the
lane is grassy-edged and wide, bordered
with tall hawthorn hedges, from which
there starts full many a top-heavy lop-
branched elm.   Such is the village, no
different from the Clintons and Bush-
worths of the neighbourhood, yet conscious
of a certain prestige.   For it is the oldest
hamlet in the township, and its trees are
the largest, and its name is Arden.

Arden lies higher than any village near.
At one extremity the road dips abruptly
down to the ford, and at the other makes
an even steeper descent.   Just at the head
of this sudden valley stands the church,
the pride of Arden   It is old and grey,
square-towered and squat, and its shadow
hallows a graveyard thick with graves :
and from this beautiful open churchyard

one looks for miles on miles, seeing the country roll away, featureless and monotonous, with never a lake nor even the bend of a stream, till at last the small irregular fields, and the lanes edged with trees, get pressed together in a dim woody line, and a ring of greenish blue vapour ends the horizon.

The view is from the back of the church. Opposite it in front stands the Hall, hidden in ash trees and tall widebranched sycamores. From the gate you could throw a pebble into the garden of the smart red-brick parsonage alongside the church. So, as there is no society in the neighbourhood, it matters much to the Rectory who lives at the Hall, and to the Hall who occupies the Rectory.

One June some years ago, after a long interval of sub-letting, the Hall had returned to the possession of its hereditary owners. A shabby happy-go-lucky house it appeared, for the Masters were poor and numerous. They were not an ideal house-hold—all the brothers and sisters quarrelled among themselves, and Mrs. Masters quar-relled with them all, and with her easy-going indolent husband more than with any other. Great was the relief when, as sometimes happened, she would leave the house in a fit of anger and shelter herself for weeks with her mother. And yet it was through her that the family had always maintained its old prestige ; it was through her that the children were neither ignorant nor destitute, and by her means the standard of morals in the home of loose-living, easy-going Jim Masters, was even rigorously pure. Yet her children were glad when she went away, and her husband dreaded her return.

Her temper was soured and indignant ; no doubt she was a difficult mistress, and she was very proud. To her it did not seem very long since she had been beautiful Kitty Arden, the toast of the county, rich, spoiled, admired, loved, everybody's darling. It did not seem very long ago, and now Catherine Masters was an unhappy woman, aged and soured, her fortune spent, her beauty faded, her children brought up in poverty and fallen from their true position. Nevertheless, when in June the Masters had come back to the Hall, the Vicar, Mr. Law, had been heartily glad to see her. He had often thought of handsome, frank Kitty Arden, for whom, in his curate days, he had cherished a secret flame. He recognised her still, even in the soured and battling woman who returned to her old home so sadly changed. He at least was always glad to see her. On the morrow of her sudden return from her mother's shelter, he would limp up to the Hall, peering through his spectacles, would fidget about the room in his timid, intimate fashion, asking after the friends she had left with an ease that robbed her absence of its tragedy. For Mr. Law never showed

that he understood the miserable civil
warfare of the Hall. His presence was
always the signal for a truce. He was the
special friend, the butt, the chum of all the
youngsters.

Besides the Vicar and the Masters
there were few persons above the rank
of farmers for many miles around. But
as two of these unvisitable households
contain the chief personages of our story,
we must step over thresholds which Mrs.
Masters never crossed ; for the better-class
farmers were both too rich and too humble
to have any acquaintance with the Hall,
and neither family knew more of the other
than the village gossip told, or the sight of
each other in church on Sundays vouch-
safed.

The Williamses were the chief farmers
in Arden. Their family had been for
generations the most respected and honourable of any in the country side. Their
house was better than the Hall—which, in

truth, was but a tumble-down and rickety
erection.   They lived about a mile from
the church, in a large black and white
half-timbered house close to the road.   On
three sides of it the orchard went ; in front
there was a tiny garden of flowers.   Harry
Williams, a man on the turn of forty, was
the most able farmer in the county.   He
looked down with great contempt on those
neighbours of his who had turned all their
fields into grazing land, and though they
all knew that the value of arable land has
decreased at the rate of 3*l*. 3*s*. an acre in the
last twenty years, Harry Williams flaunted
his golden fields of grain in the face of their
statistics, and made as good an income as
the luckiest of his forefathers.   Many a
well-to-do lass would have been proud to
rule over the ample plenty of the black
and white house ; but Harry was still un-
married.   His step-mother lived with him,
a pretty, faded, useless, falsely-elegant
ex-governess of fifty.   Her child—Harry's

step-sister, twenty-four years younger than
himself — closes the list of that house-
hold.

Half a mile further on the road to
Preston Ford you pass a white gate and a
long drive overhung with apple-trees. The
drive is the eighth of a mile in length, and
leads to a pretty rough-cast house, half
villa, half farm, nearly hidden in the roses
and ivy that clamber over the long verandah and make a huge tod on the red roof
of the porch. Here Mr. Lawrance lived.
Years ago, Mr. Lawrance of the Bushes had
been a person of importance in the restricted
society of Arden.

All that was changed now. Mr. Lawrance might not have existed for any notice
that his neighbours took of him. It must,
one would think, be a terrible delinquency
that would cause so narrow and lonely
a society to cast one member away.
But no, a second marriage had done for
him. When Mr. Lawrance first bought

the Bushes, he was a well-to-do idle county
lawyer with a wife gentle and delicate, and
an indolent handsome son. The son went
away to Paris to study art, and his mother
very sorely missed him ; she grew pale and
old ; yet in every letter she begged her
John to be industrious, not to be disheartened, to keep to his work. For she
was in spirit a woman of energy and ambi-
tion, and it was more tolerable to her to
eat out her heart in loneliness, than to con-
ceive that her only son should sink into
the passive indolence, the mere acquies-
cence with life, which distressed her in his
father. She had her reward. One summer
John Lawrance came home, a successful
painter, and brought his bride to Arden.
He had married well ; the young Mrs.
Lawrance was such a sweet, well-nur-
tured, well-behaved New Englander as
Longfellow's Priscilla must have been.
She and her mother-in-law became great
friends, and she, in her enthusiasm for the

old village, would fain have settled in Arden.
But John declared that his art required
him to live in Italy ; and his mother was
against his stagnating in a country village.
Nevertheless, having seen her children de-
part, she only lived long enough to get the
news, anxiously expected, that a grandchild
was born to her. 'We have called her
Arden Sylvia, in memory of home,' wrote
the proud and somewhat romantic mother.
Mrs. Lawrance smiled ; but she was never
well enough to answer the letter.

A few days afterwards she died—and
everyone pitied poor, lonely, Mr. Lawrance.
John, with an inward hope of refusal,
begged him to come and make his home in
Via Margutta with his children. But the
old man declared he would stick to the
old place ; and when soon after this the
younger Mrs. Lawrance died, her husband
felt his future too unsettled to press his
father to share it. The long winter rolled
away—he in Rome could not realise how

slowly to the solitary at the Bushes—and in spring the whole village of Arden, and one terzo piano in the Via Marguttta, were thunder-struck by the news of Mr. Lawrance's second marriage. He had married his housekeeper.

John Lawrance felt outraged, and the whole village more or less indignant, for the first Mrs. Lawrance was still well remembered. But the old man and his new wife were not unhappy in their unbroken solitude *à deux*. Perhaps the sense of universal disapprobation abroad made each more anxious to prove to the other that their union was not a mistake. Nor was it; for they loved each other. Yet love had come to them as a surprise; it was not in the bond. He had taken her as a provision against future helplessness; she—a woman no longer young, friendless, never beautiful—took with him friendship, a home, a future. And taking so much, she gave in proportion.

She was a woman whose native strength of feeling, whose deep capacity for attachment, devotion, vindictiveness, had long been under the control of paid and jog-trot duty. And now duty and passion were one. All the strength of her perfervid heart came out in her marriage. She was used to be paid for her service, not loved for it; she, a poor plain neglected elderly woman —and the sweet pang of this remembrance would spur her on to ever-increasing devotion and unselfishness. Mr. Lawrance was grateful. He felt he had gained a good deal more than he had bargained for, that life was sweeter to him than he had dreamed it could be at his age. Before a year was out this couple, isolated from the world in penalty for a choice made without any thought of passion, welcomed their solitude, and would have resented any change from their complete dependence on each other. And so it came to pass that Mr. Lawrance was an outlaw in the parish.

Such was the relative position of the four principal houses in Arden when my story begins. And, though a commonplace to the social observer, the mere human being cannot refrain from astonishment, considering that out of these four families in their mutual loneliness, three were absolutely dead to each other, as separate as if encompassed by a magic wall. The clergyman knew each apart, but had no power to bring them together. The Hall, the Farm, the Bushes were absolutely separate microcosms, each practically non-existent to the other two.

Such is the astonishing, yet common, position of affairs when my story begins.

CHAPTER II.

A MITHERLESS BAIRN.

WHILE these villagers drowsed away their
lives in peaceful Arden, John Lawrance
and his girl spent vivid years in Italy.
He was at this time a successful and even
eminent painter, and might be placed
third, after Fortuny and the young
Madrazo, among the brilliant realists
who, at that time, were beginning to make
their head-quarters at Rome. In every
respect, he was a fortunate painter. Not
only did he love his art and succeed in it,
but he hit the taste of the moment and the
place. He was rich, generous to extrava-
gance, popular, full of youth and a sort
of nervous exuberance that passed for

strength. Nevertheless, he did not marry
again. People in Rome explained this fact
by a fatal attachment for a beautiful Con-
tessa, much his senior, and unhappily
married. Whether it were so or not, there
were no signs of the great passion in
Lawrance's demeanour; he appeared perfectly contented with his free, occupied,
successful life, and with the society of his
little girl. She grew up a quiet, dreamy
child, with the capacity for romance which
had distinguished her mother, modified by
her father's unimpassioned facile temperament. The romance of her childhood was
Rome.

From the windows of the large, pic-
turesque studio in Via Margutta, you
looked across a network of gardens,
straight to the Pincian Hill. Right in
front of you, on the crest of the hill, rose
the grave and sombre grove of ilexes
before the Villa Medici. However hot the
sun poured down upon the grey stone

walls alive with lizards, however it glowed on the golden-burdened orange-trees, and streamed on the hedges of frail China roses till the over-blown pink petals strewed the ground, though it filled the air with the faint hawthorn-like scent of the Japanese medlars, and lay like painted gold on the walls of the houses, there was always coolness in that grove where the water of the fountain drips slowly, drop by drop, from the over-brimming cup above to the moss-covered slab below. Here Arden used to stray with her nurse, and look over the low wall to Rome lying at her feet. She used to love the place ; but one day, when she was about seven, she conceived a horror of it. Nothing had happened, only it had flitted across her mind that the shadow of death must be like this ilex-shadow, grey, cold, colourless, impenetrable to the sun. And thereafter she would play no more near the green old fountain under the gnarled branches. Such a child she was, dreamy, full of vague romantic fancies, with little real hold on life, none of the turbulence, passion, merriment of ordinary children.

As a child, this romantic sentiment for Rome quite occupied her heart. As she grew a little older she became excessively attached to her father; but, at first, she had taken him very quietly as a natural adjunct of existence. There was a sort of sweet dreamy inertness about the child, as if a shock of waking was necessary to arouse her most elementary perception. Till she was nearly seven years old her heart slept on, charmed and silent, in its palace of dreams. Then a very slight thing wakened it. It was this.

On her seventh birthday her father, who was immensely proud of his little Biondina, gave her a golden ring, the colour of her curls, he said. It was just such a ring as you may see by scores in the Piazza di Spagna; a plain hoop of gold

with on it the posy: 'Roma amor.' He
slipped it on her finger and told her to
keep it always, for soon they were going
away from Rome to Paris, and she must
always treasure it as a memorial. Little
Arden burst into a storm of tears. Was
that hoop of gold all that would remain to
her of Rome? The child was half-mad-
dened with that first anguished fear of
loss which grown people can hardly understand or remember.

As for her father, he looked upon her
tears as a child's pardonable outburst of
grief, unreasonable and soon forgotten.
But when, as the days went on, Ardenina
grew thin and paler, with a strange tense
look in the pained little white-rose face,
and when the light-blue eyes that used to
be so bright grew large and wistful, he
could not bear to see it. After all she was
all he had, this odd little girl with her
desperate love for Rome. Instead of growing angry, he was touched. And he was

more at home in the Via Margutta than
anywhere else.   It had been a mere freak,
the wish to go to Paris—and then he
thought of the moving.

'Nina,' he cried, as the pale little wretch
appeared. 'Ardenina,' he said, 'after all we
will stick to Rome, you and I.'

That piece of renunciation won for him
the passionate gratitude, the unhesitating
absolute devotion of his little girl. The
sound and look of the fountains in the
square; every sudden gay branch of ole-
ander waving over the wall; the great
round daisies in the Borghese gardens,
bending with the wind, all silver white one
way, all red the other; all these cherished
joys of Arden's childhood came to her now
as her father's gift.   And though, perhaps,
she never quite perceived his real qualities,
she would in good earnest have laid down
her baby life for this ideal father of hers.

When Arden was about eight years old
she made friends with two American chil-

dren, who, with their mother and their consumptive father, had come to winter in Rome. Winter after winter they returned, and with every year Mr. Rose grew thinner, walked slower, looked with more anxious and penetrating glances at Ellie and Gerard and Arden, as they acted all the triumphs of Rome over again in their childish play.

The girl was sharp-featured, pretty, somewhat discontented; eleven years of age. She always wore fresh smart dresses, and it was only now and then she would condescend to play with the others. Arden was a little afraid of her. She was more at home with Gerard—two years younger than his sister—a quick, observant, sweet-natured boy, with a sharp phrase and an extemporised wisdom ready to meet every emergency of life. He was never ashamed of playing with Arden; his swift intelligence and merry fancy made quite a clever thing, she used to think, of her pastimes;

as the years slipped by, till Arden in her
turn was eleven, the children left off their
games and used to visit the great temples
and museums of Rome. What Arden
loved above all, was to wander in the
galleries of the Vatican. While she was
drawing, Gerard would saunter up and
down, giving vent to fluent theories of art,
not very new perhaps or very deep, but
which Arden considered worthy of a more
brilliant Winckelmann.

But one year, when she was nearly
thirteen, when the Roses came as usual
to spend the winter in Rome, Gerard had
no heart for mirth. He could seldom talk
with Arden then, for his whole time was
spent with his father. Mr. Rose had grown
thinner than ever, and over his wasted face
there was a strange grey colour, that made
Arden think, with a shiver, of the wan ilex-
shadows.

She had always liked Mr. Rose, but
now she felt afraid of him. 'Why does he

look so strange?' she would say to herself. 'Perhaps he has done something wicked. Perhaps he has the *mal occhio*,' and she kept out of his way, slinking down some side path when she saw Gerard and his father in the distance.

But one day changed all that—one day when Gerard, trying to speak to her, could only find a voice for heavy broken sobs— 'What is it, Gerard?' she cried, alarmed; 'is it about your father?'

'Yes; one month—that's all.' Gerard could say no more.

Arden looked at him with clear, wondering eyes; it had never occurred to her that there was any danger in Mr. Rose's customary illness. She had always known him ill; Gerard's father was ill, and her father was a painter; both habits were well-known and established facts, not to be changed or questioned. Gerard saw that she did not understand. He felt hurt, angry to think that what had been grieving him so long had been quite uncomprehended by his special chum; he turned round and began speaking quite unlike himself— quite savagely, Arden fancied.

'I thought you kept out of my way because you knew I wanted to think of nothing but him now. I thought you had some sense and feeling, though you are a girl. But I guess you're all alike—you and Ellie, and all the rest; you think of nothing but yourselves. There's nothing matters to you but some new makebelieve or other; but I guess you know that my father has been in consumption all these years?'

'Yes,' said Arden, nodding her head and staring.

'Well, understand, there's no hope now.'

Arden had grown quite pale; her blue eyes were opened to their widest, but more from Gerard's roughness than from a clear understanding of his anxiety.

'*Dio Mio!*' she said, with a little shiver.

Then, coming up to the boy, who stood still glaring at her, she laid both her hands upon his arm.

'Oh, Gerard,' she cried suddenly, 'Will your father die?'

'You brute!' burst out the boy, wrenching her hands from his arm; he dashed away, leaving Arden to wonder what it all meant.

It was not very long before she learnt. She heard one day that Mr. Rose was dead, and soon after she went with her father to see Mrs. Rose and the children. They were all in black, and all, in various degrees, had the same look on their faces, the same hushed and restrained expression. Arden felt held at arm's length; a great experience was opened like a gulf between herself and her old playfellows. They had passed out of the fairyland of childhood, which she, young for her thirteen years, still wandered in. There seemed less difference, she thought, between Ellie and Gerard, and quite old people, like her father and Mrs. Rose, than between herself and these children who, a few months ago, had been her companions in a sort of Davidsbund, which necessarily excluded grown-up persons.

Arden sat perched on a chair against the wall, fidgetting with her feet ; all her pretty friendly ways had vanished in this atmosphere of constraint and strangeness. Besides, she could not forget that Gerard had called her a brute. So she sat nervously glancing from Ellie to Gerard, thinking what she ought to say, and feeling ill at ease.

The other two children sat equally silent. In the stillness, Mr. Lawrance's voice reached their corner of the room. He was speaking of her loss to Mrs. Rose.

'I can understand,' he was saying.

'It seems but yesterday since Arden's mother died. One does not forget, one only grows accustomed to always miss the thing dearest of all the world.'

Arden stared with all her eyes. Such a great sorrow! Did her father always feel it? Was Gerard feeling it now? She looked at his face, swollen and changed and pallid. She slid from her chair, and crept silently to his side.

Mrs. Rose's feeble voice did not reach to the end of the room where the three children had settled, but Arden could hear snatches of her father's answers.

'No; there is no consolation—only, believe me, when one has children . . . I am not unhappy now, you see, because I have Arden.'

Poor little Arden's heart was quite overcharged with awe and strangeness. So she had suffered this grief herself, and she herself had been a consolation, without any sense of either experience. She looked round at the pale and mournful faces, at the darkened room a little disordered with packing. It was the first time she had realised grief as a powerful and inevitable force. How changed the whole world seemed ; how little worth while it was to be proud or shy or offended in such a gloomy place !

All this time Arden was standing at the back of Gerard's chair. She came forward now, and touched him timidly on the arm; he looked up ; her face was wet with tears.

'Forgive me, Gerard,' she cried. 'Indeed I never meant to be a brute. I am so sorry ; oh, so sorry ! And to think I should have made you angry when you are so unhappy.'

Ellie stared in dumb surprise ; as for Gerard, he put his arm round her shoulder, saying kindly—

'I don't remember, Arden, dear ; but

I guess you never meant to get me mad with you.'

'You don't remember?'

That was strangest and hardest of all. Why, it was only a little time ago; and ever since Arden had kept on thinking, always, always, of this first quarrel with Gerard. She had been in a hundred minds about it—sorry, ashamed, magnanimous, proud, contrite—and Gerard had said, 'I don't remember,' as if it had all been years ago. Yes, that was just it, she thought. It was as if Gerard had suddenly grown up and left her behind. She supposed it was because his father had died.

'Gerard,' she cried, 'remember I have lost my mother, too!'

'Dear little Arden,' said the boy, 'I declare I could love to take you with us.'

'She couldn't leave her father, I presume,' put in Ellie.

'What, are you going?' cried Arden—
then, before they could answer, she understood it all, the packing, the commotion
overhead.

'At once?' she asked in a shrill little
gasp.

'That's so, Arden; we must go,' said
Gerard.

'Why, certainly,' chimed in Ellie.
'We're going home.'

'To America?' said Arden in despair,
with just such a feeling as if the dark
Tiber waters were closing above her head.

'Yes, home,' repeated Ellie.

'But we shall come back to you,
Arden,' said the boy.

'Well, I don't know about that,' Ellie
said. 'It's a long way; besides, there's no
reason now for coming. We've not been
home these five years, and I guess mother'll
be in no hurry to leave.'

Ellie's metallic little voice, with no
cruel purpose, went on deliberately, un-

feelingly, closing all the doors of the future on our poor little Arden's prison of despair. She looked up bewildered.

'Oh Gerard, is it true?'

'Well, I guess it is,' he answered.

'How strange!' said Arden, 'I wonder what it was all for?'

'What do you mean?' asked Ellie.

'I wonder why we've been such great friends, and seen each other every day; since you're going to America, you and Gerard, we shall never see each other again ever.'

'Oh yes, we shall!' cried Gerard.

'Why; anyway,' said Ellie, 'one must have friends. Living in Rome, you'll get used to knowing people passing through. That's so pleasant in Rome; people are real friendly, and make it cheerful to one while one stays.'

'Oh dear!' said Arden, holding Gerard's hand, and looking a very forlorn little person.

She did not say any more; she felt as if she did not know the language. In a few minutes Mr. Lawrance came to fetch her away. Then there were good-byes and kisses.

'You won't forget me?' said Arden.

'Never in the world,' said Gerard. 'And—let Ellie say what she likes—we'll come back, Arden.'

Arden had plenty to think of that evening, as she walked home with her father over the Pincio, where the band was playing and the people were promenading watching the sunset. The sky was all crimson and yellow, with overhead a field, as it were, of vivid luminous blue. Against this brilliant splendour, the pine-surmounted hills, the towers and domes rose up thin and shadowy; St. Peter's itself looked like a thin round of smoked glass, even St. Peter's. Then, quite suddenly as it seemed, the great ball of fire slipped behind the houses; and for a moment or two the sky blazed with ever-increasing brilliance; then, as if someone withdrew the light that illuminates a transparence, the life went out of the colours; they faded; the sky again grew distant and unnoticeable; the houses and mountains were the real things now, the things to be looked at.

Arden did not reason her fancies to a conclusion, but she felt that something of the same sort had taken place in her life All the glory had left her sky; even Rome, as it lay at her feet, looked dark, formless, a mere chaotic mass of gloomy houses.

'For I know I shall never, never get to make friends of people passing through,' she muttered between her teeth.

'What's the matter, Arden? I'm sorry you'll lose your friends, darling,' said her father, squeezing the cold little hand.

'You must be all my friends now, papa,' whispered Arden, nestling closer to his side.

It happened as Arden had said. She made no new friends to replace those she had lost, though she and her father were popular in Rome, so that Arden lived anything but a lonely life. As she grew out of childhood into girlhood, it was found that she became almost beautiful, tall, with large clear eyes, a graceful curly head, delicate flexile lips that smiled upwards. She became the darling of all the old ladies in Rome ; her father's friends, artists chiefly, over-praised her drawing because she was so pretty, and John Lawrance's only girl. No young woman could have had a more social, easy, and even triumphant life. But Arden had few companions of her own age ; and among all her admirers and protectors no special friend.

Therefore she never found it hard to quit Rome, as often happened, almost at a moment's notice, to go on some impromptu sketching tour with her father. He went alone, sometimes, if the place was very rough or a difficult journey, but most often he and Arden would roam together to some Castello on the visible spurs of the Alban or the Sabine hills.

Nothing delighted Arden more than these impromptu journeys. She had the passion of all foreigners for the desolate Campagna; the passion which true Romans so little understand. Besides these flying visits, there was, of course, the necessary four months' absence in the summer. Then they would go to Umbria or Tuscany; sometimes, even to Switzerland or the Tyrol; but to England never.

To Arden it seemed almost impossible to realise that she herself was English, and had relations in England, her only relations, who had never been in Italy.

'As for me, you know,' she would say, 'I should die of the cold and fog, and of sheer longing for Rome.'

And then a shadow would settle for a moment on her father's sunny face, and he would make no answer.

Every Christmas Eve Arden wrote to her grandfather, whom she had never seen, sending him some sketch, some piece of embroidery, something done by her own hands as a Christmas gift. In return she would get a few lines of thanks, and this was all the correspondence that ever passed between them. But one year, when Arden was just seventeen years old, her father came into the garden one warm May morning, and said,

'Arden, I think this year we had better go to England.'

'Oh, papa!'

'Why, dear? You have never been in England; I will take you to Arden, to your namesake village. Your mother used to think it more beautiful than Italy; it is so fresh and green.'

'Oh papa, I shall hate it!' exclaimed Arden. 'But of course we will go if you like.'

'Why would you hate it? That is silly, Arden. England is our own country after all; I often think I should like to see it again.'

'Oh, if you want, of course, papa.'

'You don't know what it's like, Arden,' he said, drawing her to his side and keeping his arm round her shoulder; 'those green villages, the red little thatched houses nestling under great oaks and elms; the green where the geese feed and the boys play cricket, with a pond at one end for the ducks; the village inn with its swinging sign; the red-cheeked, comely villagers, who all know you, with whom you have a place to fill by rights; not a stranger, a foreigner as you are here.'

'A foreigner in Rome, I? It's in England I should be a foreigner, papa.'

'Besides, I think you ought to know

more of your grandfather. Your home would be with him, should anything happen to me.'

'Don't, don't, dear,' cried Arden, throwing her arms round her father's neck and half stifling him with kisses. 'You are young and he is old. How could it be ? But I'll go to England.'

'Well, well; there's no need to settle yet ; we'll think about it, dear.'

The more Arden thought about going to England the less she liked the idea. Suppose when they once got to England, her father should refuse to come back ? This was a sort of nightmare to the girl, who had known some people who, having lived ten years in Rome, had gone home for a summer visit and had settled there.

Then the various old ladies whom Arden made her confidants would try to comfort her, finishing their consolations with a little well-meant sermon on un-selfishness and sacrifice, and the duty of daughters. So Arden would go home, dignified with a temporary patience and resignation. She would ask her father, with an Iphigenia air, whether she should dismiss all the servants and when he meant to start; she would try to take an interest in England, asking forlorn little questions about the journey and the climate.

John Lawrance felt his resolution giving way. He had always given in to Arden, because it cost him so much to make her give in to him. He had resolved on this English visit; since he felt it would be for Arden's benefit to make acquaintance with the relations who would be her guardians in the event of his own death. But after all he was still a young man, not more delicate than many ; it was probable, as the child had said, that he would outlive his father. Nor could his old home, re-visited under such changed conditions, be productive of aught but painful memories to him. When he had seen it last, his

wife was with him, his mother alive.
Now there would be a haunting emptiness
in every spot ; and, worst of all, he would
have to face the detested upstart step-
mother. For Arden's sake he would have
borne it all ; but the child did not wish
it—perhaps the visit, after all, was ill
advised.

Matters were in this condition, when,
about three weeks after the question began
to be debated, Arden entered her father's
studio one day, radiant, an open letter in
her hand.

' Oh, papa, fancy. What do you think ? '

' I'm sure I don't know, dear. Something pleasant ? '

' The Roses are coming to Venice this
summer. Coming in the end of June.'

' The Roses ? Oh, your American
friends. Well, I'm very glad, Arden.'

' So of course we can't go to England
this year ? '

' No ; I suppose that settles it. I

suppose you'll want to go to Venice, eh,
dear ?'

' Oh, papa.'

Arden danced all over the room, all
over the house for sheer joy. Her father
was painting her that morning in a white
dress, against a sunny white wall, the
sweet brilliant face and golden head the
only spot of colour in the picture. He
caught the look of dazzled joy upon her
face, the abandon and alertness of youth in
the poise of her figure ; the picture was
his master-piece, and created quite a sensation in Rome. It still remains that picture,
that incarnation of eager fearless youth.
When it was painted it was very like
Arden Lawrance.

It was all arranged that they should
go to Venice. Arden took all the trouble
on herself, hired the apartments, engaged
servants ; so that her father found himself
at home in Venice almost as completely
as in Rome. As for Arden, all this time

she was wild with joy and expectation, she
laughed, and talked, and sang all day, and
then railed at the days for passing so
slowly. (Ah, happy days pass slowly.)
'And it is still more than a fortnight to
the end of June!'

'Terrible interval! I must leave you
to bear a few days of it in solitude, too, my
girl.'

'Why, papa, are you going away?
May I not go with you?'

'No, dear; I want to paint the Campo
at Torcello. I shall put up with the priest;
but that would hardly do for you. Moreover, is not Torcello a desolate feverish
place, with nothing to eat but pomegranates,
and nowhere to sleep but ruins?'

'Well, mind you don't take the fever,
papa. It would be too ignominious, after
living twenty years in Rome, to get
malaria at Torcello. Must you go to-
morrow?'

'To-morrow morning, I think.'

' Then I ought to go now and tell Gigi
to put you up some things. *A rivederei!*'
and she ran away, a light white figure
across the dark cortile.

After her father was gone to Torcello,
Arden was quite alone. It had been
arranged that she should leave him four
days to work at his background, and that
on the fifth Gigi should punt her out in the
gondola to fetch her father home. The
first two days lagged and dragged away ;
it is difficult to be merry alone, away from
home, with nothing to do. Arden was not
merry, but neither was she sad. She
dreamed over again her Roman childhood,
all the years of it at least that she had
played away with the Roses ; and then she
fabricated an imaginary future in which
Mrs. Rose settled in Rome, and Arden and
Gerard and Ellie were bound together in
perfect companionship. But after a while
the pleasantest dreams cease to satisfy.
They are like the fairy gold which glitters

all night, but turns, when the sun shines on
it, to dust and withered leaves.

On the third morning of her loneliness,
the sun shone on Arden's reveries; the
world outside looked white and hazy blue,
and brilliant and pure as only Venice
can look, and only Venice on a hot and
rather misty morning. Arden went out,
walked through the narrow Calles, over the
steep arched bridges, into the great white
square of St. Mark; at the end the golden
cupolas shone out all yellow and burning
in the sunshine.

Arden went inside. They were singing
an office at the altar. In the choir and in
the smaller chapels little separate flocks of
women knelt and prayed. In the nave five
artists stood or sat in separate spots, painting at their easels. Nearer the door some
women, who had been marketing in the
Merceria, were resting their heavy baskets
on the benches, and talking volubly to a
white-shirted gondolier. All over the

church people were living, not as in a church, but as in a happy meeting-place where each did as he liked best; some talked, some walked, some sang, some prayed, some merely rested. For St. Mark's is the true abbey of Thelema.

Arden's choice was to pass out of the busy nave into one of the many little chapels, placed some high upstairs, some down. She used to like, when she was tired or lonely, to get into such a quiet nook, to sit in the gloom on a slab of red marble, and look out at the light and colour of the church, at the beautiful arches, the golden mosaics, the deeply-coloured marbles, red, green, and blue, the Byzantine pictures, solemn or grotesque. To get to her favourite chapel it was necessary to turn sharply round by the rail of the chancel. Here there are always a good many people, some watching the service, some trying to see the mosaics on the ceiling. Arden, her white dress clear in the darkness, her hands crossed lightly in front of her waist, came up the twilit nave and stood a moment at the corner, her head thrown back, smiling a little, wondering if it would be possible to pass. As she stood thus, a ray of light caught her golden curls, her white dress. An elegant, sharp-featured young woman leaning on the rail, half-turned towards her, then turned altogether; her pretty grey eyes opened in a stare.

'Why mother, why Gerard,' she exclaimed shrilly, 'I declare if it isn't Arden Lawrance!'

An older lady, plump, richly dressed, with an elaborate coiffure; a handsome, velvet-jacketed, nonchalant youth, with a sort of restrained eagerness under his nonchalance; and with the appearance of having fine manners but not good breeding, all came forward with outstretched hands.

'Why, Arden dear!' cried Mrs. Rose.

'Won't you shake hands?' said Gerard.

She was standing, her hands still

clasped before her, a perplexed little smile
hovering round her mouth. Gerard thought
he would like to paint her; she had certainly grown very pretty; but why did she
look so unreal and dreamy? Had she forgotten them? Gerard, who to tell the
truth had not often thought of his childish
playfellow during their long separation, felt
a sudden desire to be on terms of intimacy
with this slim white girl, whose shining
eyes and bright curls were beautiful even
in the dim light of the church.

'Won't you shake hands?' he said
again; a little piqued by her silence.

'Oh, is it really you!' she cried, looking at all the three faces in turn. 'How
good of you to come so soon!'

'Yes, it is we!' said Gerard smiling;
it was clear, then, that she did remember.

'It has been such a long time!' said
the girl, half-crying, half-laughing, press-
ing their hands as if to make sure they
were real.

'Hush, Arden dear, don't cry!' said
Mrs. Rose; 'don't be so excited, my child.
Remember we're in church!'

'No, I won't cry.' After a moment she
looked at them, including them all in her
sweet wistful smile, that made an apology
of her words. 'Of course it's different
to you,' she said. 'You have so many
friends. I know I am very silly. But
I didn't expect to see you for three
weeks!'

'I declare you haven't altered in the
least all these years,' cried Ellie, who
thought Arden always too much given to
making a fuss.

'Like the Bourbons?' Arden smiled.
'At any rate I've forgotten nothing!'

'No; she is not altered in the least,'
cried Gerard. 'She was always the dearest
girl in the world!'

Arden smiled. 'Ellie's altered,' she
said. 'Do come into the light, Ellie; I
want to see how pretty you have grown!'

'I think Ellie might retort,' cried Gerard.

'And I think,' joined in Mrs. Rose, 'that if you young people can't keep quiet, you had better go out of church.'

'Mother!' cried Ellie, shocked at so much reverence; 'one would think you had never been outside Massachusetts!'

'And it's not a church,' put in Gerard.

'Church or chapel, it's a place of worship,' decided Mrs. Rose.

Arden looked on wondering. She saw no reason why one should not talk in church. But now Gerard began again, and the little drawl he spoke with seemed to exaggerate itself as he talked.

'A place of worship!' he cried with an air of somewhat faded and languid enthusiasm. 'That is precisely what this place is not. Look round: all these people, chattering, flirting, chatting, sight-seeing; are they worshippers? It was not built to worship in, this splendid, fantastic, irregu-

lar Temple of Colour, dim and glowing,
incoherently coherent like a dream. I will
tell you what it is ; a sign to Heaven of the
triumph of the world, a flaunting in the
eyes of God of the pomps and lusts of
princes. And the decadent East has con-
quered Christ in this mosque raised to his
name, yet tainted with the gorgeous sin,
yet hallowed with the unholy beauty of
Venice Meretrix ! '

'Gerard !' cried Arden. 'Oh don't
you remember how you used to go on
about the Guilia in the Braccio Nuovo ? '

' "Go on !" Little Goth ! If that is
how you blaspheme my æsthetic theories, I
shall stop. I shall suit my conversation to
my hearers.'

' Ah ! And what will you do ? '

' I shall be natural,' said Gerard.

Meanwhile Mrs. Rose and Ellie had
been looking round the church.

' Dear me !' said the girl ; ' what a
great many people painting, to be sure ! '

'I call it sheer irreverence!' cried Mrs. Rose. 'And during service too!'

'Don't be too hard upon them, mother,' said her son. 'Next week you will have to be equally shocked at me.'

'Oh, can you paint as well as talk?' cried Arden.

'I can paint,' said Gerard; 'but not as well as I talk.'

'If you can paint at all, I am glad; for now you can go out sketching with papa.'

'What a flattering scheme for getting me out of the way! But I haven't seen Mr. Lawrance yet,' continued Gerard, looking round.

'Papa! What a shame to have forgotten him all this time. He is at Torcello, painting the Campo.'

'Torcello; that's the Early Christian island I've put down in our Itinerary,' said Ellie.

'Ah, to think it is near!' mused her brother. 'To me it has always seemed the

Ultima Thule of deserted Fairyland, that
weird and fever-stricken Basilica, mid-seas ;
the abandoned mother of dissolute, thank-
less Venice.'

'Fever-stricken ! ' echoed Mrs. Rose.
'Oh Arden, you've never let your father
go there alone ! '

'I am afraid I have. You see I had
no choice ; he said he must go and I must
stay ; so there was nothing to do ! '

'Mercy ! How European,' cried Ellie
in her sharp little voice. 'In our country
a young woman does what she thinks
right ; she's a responsible being every
time ! '

'But you see, Ellie, I don't know what
suits papa. And I don't think he will get
the fever ; we're Romans, you know. Besides he has only been there two days, and
on Thursday I am going in the gondola
to fetch him home.'

'I suppose you keep a gondola of your
own ? ' inquired Ellie.

'Well,' said Mrs. Rose. 'I can't feel easy about that fever.'

''Tis strange,' assented Gerard. ''Tis the universal revenge of Antiquity. We desert her great cities and insult her empire, and when at last we return and would acknowledge her, she poisons us——'

'Torcello's not antique,' cried Ellie, Baedeker in hand. 'It's a question of drainage, I guess.'

Gerard did not seem to hear her. He continued vaguely, 'Once the Mother of Faith, now a deserted poisonous Fairyland. It would'—he went on more seriously—'make a splendid metaphor if I could only think of something to compare it to.'

Meanwhile Arden was speaking eagerly to the elder lady—

'Dear Mrs. Rose, won't you all go with me to Torcello on Thursday? Think how surprised and delighted papa would be! And you will have to see the island——'

'Why certainly,' chimed in Ellie, who evidently managed affairs. 'I guess we can fix it up together. We are bound to visit all the sights, and you can show us round, I presume.'

'Thank you, Ellie. I'm so glad; you will come too, Gerard, won't you? Yes, you must bring your sketching block. Oh, fancy, how surprised papa will be!' Arden broke into a little, silvery, child's laugh of delight.

'Well,' said Mrs. Rose, 'I think it's a good plan. And now, as you're all alone, Arden, you must spend the day with us, we'll lunch at Florian's.'

'Ah, yes, the historic Florian!' murmured Gerard, pushing back his hair.

'What's that?' asked Ellie, touching Arden's arm and pointing. Arden shivered.

It was only a procession of poor old men in faded crimson; some of them holding candles, some censors, some a black-palled coffin; each and all swinging their

burdens somewhat roughly. It was a pauper's funeral. They placed the coffin rather
hurriedly upon a bier that had been standing, unnoticed, waiting for the dead. At
this moment the foot of one of the bearers
slipped upon the uneven pavement, and he
stumbled, letting go his hold. The other
three old men pushed the coffin into its
proper place.

Arden turned a little pale, Gerard
saw it.

'I feel with you,' he whispered, 'that
that neglected pauper's sorrow is the di-
vinest thing in this marvel of a church.'

'I don't know how I feel,' said Arden,
'suddenly cold and wicked, I think; we
were so happy. Perhaps a cock has crowed
on my grave.'

Then they went out to lunch at
Florian's.

CHAPTER III.

THERE'S NOTHING HALF SO SWEET IN LIFE.

'I AM sure you would not forget Torcello, Mrs. Rose.'

The sentence came from Arden, in answer to an excuse from Thursday's expedition, in which the elder lady pleaded her bad memory for sights.

'My dear girl, I have forgotten the Apollo Belvedere, and the Sistine Chapel, and the Joconde. Now in Boston, they assured me if I could forget Joconde I could forget anything, and Gerard, he seems to suppose the same.'

'Torcello is much lovelier that the Joconde.'

'Well, that's pretty far-fetched, I guess,

comparing a picture and a place!' cried
Ellie.

'Yet they have both the same melancholy, supersensuous charm.' This last
remark came from Gerard, who was sketching in the window.

'That dome is out of drawing,' observed
Arden, looking over his shoulder ; then, as
she turned round, 'But even if you did
forget it, Mrs. Rose, you would enjoy it at
the time.'

'Gather ye roses while ye may,'
hummed the young man ; 'what does it
matter if they are not the best sort for pot
pourri!'

· Gerard always tags on a meaning to
my argument,' laughed Arden, 'like the
moral in italics at the end of the fable.'

'Which no one reads or heeds,' he
added.

'You young people would have a
better time by yourselves,' cried Mrs. Rose,
showing her trumps at this juncture.

'Oh no, indeed. It is because you are here we are so merry! And we shall have to take two gondolas because of papa's things; so there is plenty of room.'

'And mother could return with the easels; capital arrangement!'

'It was Gerard, you know, Mrs. Rose, who pretended there was no room. Can you not really go?'

'No, my dear, I think not.'

'I'm so sorry.'

'What a fidget you are, Arden,' cried Ellie, 'let mother go her way and we'll go ours. Elderly folks don't like to be dragged around seeing sights.'

'I'm sorry,' said the girl again; 'it's settled then.'

'Yes; that's fixed,' decided Ellie, 'and now, Arden and Gerard, I want to go round the Ducal Palace.'

'Not I,' said Gerard, 'this work of art is more precious to me just now than all the paradise of Tintoret.'

'Well, I don't believe I shall find the way.'

'I'm ready,' said Arden.

'What!' cried the young man, 'without one single protest do you submit yourself to the yoke of Ellie's chariot? What a lack of wisdom and proper spirit! I suppose I must come too, then.'

'And leave the work that is more than Tintoret?'

'But I never said more than Arden.'

They went along through brilliant, silent Venice, to the white court of the palace, through the lines of gallery that so wonderfully catch up and repeat the colours of the outer world, sea-blue and sky-green, crimson and yellow and scarlet and purple of the fruit-laden barges, silvery tones of distance and of mist.

Even Ellie was awakened to enthusiasm.

'It's just as lovely as it can be!' she cried, as they slowly descended the outer staircase.

Gerard roused himself from an abstracted silence.

'Yes, that's so,' he answered; 'such hair and eyes!'

Arden stared. Ellie frowned, and said nothing.

Indeed, during those days Ellie had much cause for frowning. She even confided her fears to her mother.

'Well, I presume, my dear,' said Mrs. Rose, 'you will think him in love with a baby next. The child has no manners at all.'

'That, I fear,' said Ellie, 'is just what Gerard admires.'

'I dare say, in a child like Arden Lawrance. Not in a woman to fall in love with.'

'Well; I don't believe but what he is falling in love with her!'

'And I believe he is not. He admires —all men do—something more deliberately engaging, attractive, fascinating. Remember Miss De la Rue.'

'I remember !'

'Boy as he is, he would have married her if she would have had him!'

'All the more reason that he should be dead in love with Arden Lawrance.'

'But what am I to do, Ellie ?' cried her mother.

'At least you must come with us everywhere ; to the galleries ; to Torcello. You should not throw them together, Mother ; it's very American. You should take us about more, and make Arden talk to you every time.'

'Oh dear !' Mrs. Rose looked out of the window. The air was quivering with the intense heat ; the roof steamed ; at the ferry a few gondoliers lay asleep in their boats ; the sun blazed whitely, its rays struck like swords.

'It is much too hot!' sighed Mrs. Rose.

'Too hot for Gerard to fall in love !' cried Ellie, with emphatic sarcasm.

'Too hot for me to endeavour to prevent him!'

Mrs. Rose sank back in her cushions, and took up her work. Ellie gazed at her one moment, a picture of energy baffled by the *vis inertia*; and then might be heard in the next room pulling out drawers with decision, as she dressed herself to go to the Lido with her brother and Arden.

Afterwards when they had escorted Arden home, she said to him,

'Why do you spoil that child with your ridiculous compliments?'

'Because she is not to be spoiled.'

'It is not fair. She will be fancying you are in love with her.'

'Not at all; she will fancy we are two children on the Pincio.'

'Or you will be falling in love with her yourself?'

'*Chi lo sa!*'

'It would be a shame; it would be ridiculous; you are both too young; you

will have no career ; you will never get
your basis. Gerard, you must not marry
yet !'

'Excellent adviser !'

'But are you in love with her, Gerard?'

'Not yet !'

CHAPTER IV.

AT THE BUSHES.

In the weedy garden at the Bushes, on one fine morning, Mr. Lawrance was walking in the temperate sunshine. He had been out but little, for the summer was late and chill, and he hobbled feebly, leaning on a stick, from flower-bed to flower-bed, inspecting the scanty annuals and the gilly-flowers all run to stalk. He was bent, and walked heavily, yet without decision ; but his white hair was thick yet, and his aquiline face was bronzed with many summers to a red brown that neither sickness nor seclusion blanched.

The sun was hot, and the old gentle-man but little used to exercise ; besides, some over-careful, loving hand had wrapped him round too closely in warm woollen wraps. He had scarcely made the tour of the half-dozen scattered beds in front of the house, before a sudden giddiness seized him. He tottered, stooped, and called out, 'Annie! here!'

His voice was feeble as his pause, but the faint echo had scarcely caught it before a dark figure, seated in the shadow of the porch, rose, let fall some work, and ran out lightly to his aid.

As she leads him homewards, with tender helpful words and gesture, let us glance at the second Mrs. Lawrance. She was a tall thin woman of fifty, flat-faced, small-featured, her pale complexion pitted and thickened by small-pox, her hair was colourless and light, her leaden-grey eyes without movement or sparkle. Even in her youth she could have had no pretension to be called pretty ; yet the face would have been an interesting study for a painter ; of its sad contour, patient eyes, long up-turned nose, thin cheeks, thin mouth with a restrained piteous pout in the upper lip, he might have made a pendant to that portrait by Raffaelle, sometimes called Maddalena Doni, which hangs in the tribune of the Uffizzi.

Just now we see Mrs. Lawrance at her best, as she stands looking on while her husband rests on the wide bench in the ivy-covered porch.

' You're 'most overdone with the 'eat, aren't you, dear ?' she says, stooping down to take off his goloshes.

She speaks loudly, for Mr. Lawrance is going deaf, and speaks with a twang which ruins her voice as the small-pox has ruined her face.

' Yes, yes,' he answers with weary impatience. ' I'm getting an old man, a broken-up old man, and a June morning is too much for me. Ah, well ! '

He looks down at his wife kneeling

with the goloshes in her hand, and goes on
to quote—

'A lean and slippered pantaloon.

' There's another scene to come yet, you
know, Annie. Second childishness, and
mere oblivion!'

Mrs. Lawrance had risen, and stood
looking at him with a sort of alarmed
affection ; always her expression when her
husband gave way to moods she could not
understand. And these, alas, were so many
moods that he, careful not to vex her, had
gradually receded, step by step, from his
old points of view, his accustomed standing-
place of thought, and had ended by con-
tenting himself with her level. So now,
when he caught her look, he changed his
tone and said,

' Well, well, Annie, there's nothing to
mind . . . . I think I'll take my medicine
now. Aye! help me in to the sofa ; I'll
rest a bit, and then we'll go and see when
the red calf 'll be fit for the butcher.'

He had already risen, and was taking his wife's arm, when, glancing out at the bright garden, he saw the postman coming up the drive.

'Why, it's Saturday, this morning, to be sure!' he exclaimed. 'I declare I had quite forgotten; my old head gets so weak. Run, Annie, and fetch the Birmingham paper; I'll wait here.'

It is descriptive of the Bushes that it was not one of those houses where, on summer mornings, the postman is treated to milk or cyder, so he was defrauded of nothing by Mrs. Lawrance's hastening to meet him on the drive. In a moment she was back with her husband in the porch.

'Here's the paper, dear,' she said. She stopped and looked at him anxiously for a moment, then she went on in a slow clear voice—

'There's summat else, dear, beside the paper; there's a letter, a furrin letter, with a black edge, and it's not in Arden's

hand ; happen summat's come to the child,
or——'

'There, there, give it me,' cried the old
man impatiently. 'Nay ! it's not John's
writing either. It's nothing at all, no
doubt, nothing at all. You women folk
are always so full of whims and fancies.'

His hand trembled so, nevertheless,
that he could scarcely break the seal. As
he read, his face took a drawn and haggard
expression. His wife drew near, and
while she laid her arm round his shoulders
to support him, looked over his shoulder at
the open letter.

This is what she read :—

'Casa Monier, Venice, June 14th.

'My dear Sir,—It is with the sincerest
sorrow and fellow-feeling that I break to
you the melancholy news of the unexpected. death of your son, and our valued
friend, Mr. John Lawrance. Your granddaughter, Arden, has begged me, as her
oldest friend, to write to you in her stead,

for the poor child does not seem to comprehend what it is necessary to say.

'When we arrived here, Mr. Lawrance had been painting for some days at an island near Venice, Torcello, and on Thursday the 12th, two days after our arrival, Arden and my son and daughter set out to fetch him home. They found him seriously ill with marsh fever, lying in a sort of hovel, with no kind of accommodation for his needs. Mr. Lawrance, who between the accesses of fever, was perfectly conscious, and even approximately well, determined to go back with the young people, and overruled all his daughter's very strenuous objections. Indeed, I presume it was impossible, from what my son has told me, that he should be left, or Arden allowed to remain, in such a feverish and squalid hole. My children returned at once to Venice with orders that all should be ready for his arrival, and I was waiting with them at

your son's house when, about eight o'clock,
Mr. Lawrance and Arden came home.
He was in a dead swoon, and for some
time altogether lifeless. When he awoke
he was in a burning fever, complicated with
acute inflammation of the lungs ; but he
retained perfect possession of his senses
until he passed away, quietly at the last,
yesterday night about half-past twelve
o'clock. I will not affect to ignore, my
dear Sir, that there has been of late a certain estrangement between you and your
son ; but, believe me, all remembrance of
it was forgotten on his death-bed. He fre-
quently spoke of you in terms of sincere affection, and of your home, regretting that
he had not gone to England this summer, as
he intended in the spring. But the greatest
proof of his entire confidence in your love
is that he has left you guardian of his very
dear and lovely daughter Arden. She will
have but a slender fortune, scarcely enough
to live upon, even in the narrowest way,

and this is tied up in such a manner that she cannot touch it until she be of age ; she is but recently seventeen. We shall be anxious to hear when it will suit you to assume your guardianship over Arden ; until then she will remain our welcome and much-loved guest. Nor need you feel as if she were thrust upon you, for though it was Mr. Lawrance's last and anxious de- sire that she should live under your roof, still in case from any cause you should find it inconvenient to accept this charge, another arrangement could doubtless take the place of this. Arden sends you her love, and believe me, dear Sir, with sincere and heartfelt sympathy,   Yours truly,

'EMILY ROSE.'

'What shall you do, dear ?' asked Mrs. Lawrance, with anxious eyes.

'Poor John ! poor fellow !' murmured the old man. 'So he has gone first after all.'

'Them as don't honour a good father, can expect no different,' replied his wife, who could be as unforgiving to her enemies as she was tender to those she loved.

'Nay, nay, Annie, the poor boy's dead now, and he was a good man in the main, was John.'

Mrs. Lawrance contented herself with looking a negative.

'And what shall you do about his darter, dear?' she asked.

'Poor child; of course she must come home; it will be very dull for her with us old folks, I fear.'

'If she's got any heart, she ought to be grateful to her kind grandpa for giving her a roof to shelter her.'

'It's not like you, Annie, to be so hard, especially when people are in trouble.'

'I'll do my best to make her happy, poor girl—but she'll be sadly in the way.'

'Ah well! And to think John should be the first to go.'

They turned through the farmyard gate together, not too much shaken to examine the red calf.

CHAPTER V.

THE MASTERS OF ARDEN.

THE news of Arden's coming rapidly spread through the village, and many were the guesses hazarded regarding the old gentleman's granddaughter. She was not envied ; much pity was bestowed on her by the young people of the village, who regarded her isolated and removed condition as the granddaughter of one of the quality, whom the quality did not know, with a peculiar mingling of contempt and longing.

Meanwhile the young 'quality' at the Hall, who were bored to death with their ancestral dignities after their free-and-easy social life at Leamington and Scarboro', looked for Arden's coming as one looks for a star on a dark night—not day-light, but still a light. They laid plots and conspiracies to persuade their mother that, though of course she could not be expected to visit the old Lawrances, still the new Miss Lawrance had done nothing to forfeit her position, and might be encouraged to visit at the Hall. And, notwithstanding her pride, Mrs. Lawrance had been induced to make a half-promise, to the effect that if she were pleased with Arden's appearance, she would leave a card for her at the Bushes and ask her to tea at the Hall.

Things had been carried to this quasi-successful issue, when one fine morning, Georgina, the second girl, set out to accompany her mother on a visit to some poor people in the village. As they passed the gate the lodgewoman had come out to offer an acceptable morsel of gossip, and with a certain pride in her superior information, told Mrs. Masters that young Miss

Lawrance was expected at the Bushes that week.

'Oh, mother, you *will* go and call on her?' implored Georgina.

'My dear child,' said her mother, 'I shall do what I consider right, and what that may be I cannot tell at present.'

'They do say, mum, as she's expected every day,' said the lodgekeeper with a sense of humble authority on the topic.

'*She!* indeed. I think, Mrs. Gay, you had better meddle no more in your betters' affairs until you know how to speak of them with respect. Ignorant impertinence!' and Mrs. Masters passed out of the gate into the lane, drawing up her long neck in disdain. Georgina walked by her side, rebelliously silent. She dared not contradict her mother; she was determined not to be over-ridden. While her mother was still intent on Mrs. Gay's iniquities, the child espied the Rector standing in the churchyard, in conversation with a boy who had driven a flock of sheep to graze upon the graves.

'Mamma, I am going to speak to Mr. Law,' she said, and ran ahead. She soon reached the lank, gaunt Rector, still midway in his lecture.

'Mr. Law,' cried Georgina, breathless, 'do come and persuade mamma to call on Miss Lawrance. She doesn't mind for anyone but you.'

The Rector turned, letting down his arm, and the boy seized the occasion for escape. Mrs. Masters was to be seen nearing the gate with a relaxing severity upon her face.

'Well, well, my dear,' said Mr. Law, 'but you shouldn't interrupt people. However, I will come and speak to your mother.'

Mrs. Masters had already reached them.

'So that child of mine is plaguing you

as usual,' she said, and held out a friendly hand.

' She is anxious to be told about Miss Lawrance.'

' To be told about! Have you seen her ?'

' Only her likeness. She must be a singularly attractive young woman I should judge, and therefore an additional plea-santness in the society of our neighbour-hood.'

The Rector dropped his words like pearls, impressively distinct. He rounded the period with a benevolent smile.

' Decidedly a welcome addition,' he re-peated.

' There, mamma !' cried Georgina, triumphing too soon.

' We shall see what we shall see,' said Mrs. Masters. 'No watering-place attrac-tions for me. I believe the girl has had no settled home.'

' On the contrary, my dear friend, she

has resided all her life in Rome under the guardianship of her father, an accomplished artist.'

' And none too respectable, I dare say.'

'Well, well! *De mortuis nil nisi bonum* ; and I have heard nothing to the late Mr. Lawrance's disadvantage.'

Which was quite true, for the Rector had seldom heard of him at all.

' In Rome!' murmured Georgina; awed, impressed, with vague recollections of Romulus and Horatius Cocles, Mrs. Mangnall and bad marks, circling in her mind.

' But to return to Miss Lawrance,' continued the Rector, ' her grandfather has shown me the letter of a friend of hers, a lady of good American family.'

' There's no such thing!' snapped Mrs. Masters.

' Well, well, my dear friend, an American lady, who describes Miss Lawrance as a person of amiable character and elegant accomplishments.'

'But I thought she was a girl!' cried poor Georgina, aghast.

'So, my dear young friend, she appears to be in point of years. In fact, I should say a most suitable companion; but she has had the advantages of a continuous residence in the most ancient capital city of Europe. She speaks, I imagine, Italian, French, and probably German; has had, no doubt, the benefit of Italian masters in singing and dancing—in fact——'

'If she's quite respectable, I'll engage her to give the girls some lessons,' said Mrs. Masters.

'Oh mamma! thank you, mamma; oh, you dear old Rector!' shouted Georgina; 'and she is only a girl, really?'

'Seventeen.'

'And pretty?'

'I should imagine most prepossessing.'

'What's her Christian name?'

Mr. Law reddened a little and cleared his throat.

It was, in fact, a very awkward question.
The good-natured Rector was anxious to
infuse a more friendly spirit into the young
people under his care ; he would be very
glad for the young Masters to be kind to
Miss Lawrance of the Bushes ; it was
the first step towards the better order of
things. But all would be lost if Mrs.
Lawrance learned—as the Rector had
learned—that young Miss Lawrance was
christened Arden. She would consider it
a vile infringement of her rights ; he did
not care even to imagine her indignation.
Nor was there any need she should ever
know it. The Rector, after revolving the
important affair over many an evening
pipe, had determined—for the sake of peace
—to entreat Mr. Lawrance to call his granddaughter by her second name if she had
one, or to invent some plausible pet name.
It could have been so easily arranged, if
only Georgina had held her tongue. And
now must he tell the truth—should he

feign ignorance or invent some chance, harmless 'Mary' or 'Sarah' for the occasion?

'What is her name?' repeated Georgina.

'Why—Lawrance—of course,' said the Rector—'Lawrance—you know her father was old Mr. Lawrance's son—the painter you know. Let's see—do you sketch, Georgina?—'

'But I mean her Christian name!' cried the incorrigible girl.

'Her name,' said the Rector with the accent of despair, 'her name is Arden.'

'What!' cried Mrs. Masters.

'Arden,' stammered the Rector—crestfallen as a guilty thing. It was even worse than he feared.

'Oh,' cried Mrs. Masters bitterly, 'this is an end of the business. Now you know, Georgina, what sort of an acquaintance you rashly wished to make. The impertinence of that upstart attorney, the insolence to palm off my family name upon his foreign granddaughter! Oh, the underbred fellow, he should be sent out of the parish—I should like to have him thrashed. Arden, indeed! A fine Arden! It's a degradation, I say. It's a slap in the face.'

'But, dear Mrs. Masters, consider,' implored the Rector, 'it is only an instance of Mr. Lawrance's bad taste. The girl did not choose her name.'

'This is a private matter, Mr. Law, and not to be argued,' cried Mrs. Masters, with tremendous dignity. 'I am the only judge of this insult, and I consider it a blow never to be forgiven. A blow, a theft I should say, the theft of my ancestral name.' She stopped for a moment, catching her breath painfully.

'Compose yourself, my dear friend,' cried the Rector in genuine alarm.

'Thank heaven, I never did compose myself when the honour of my family was at stake!' burst out Mrs. Masters with renewed acrimony. 'No, I am incapable of forgiving such an injustice. Listen, Georgina, I forbid you to do so much as speak in the lanes to that girl!'

'Oh mother,' wailed Georgina, 'how can you be so unjust!'

'Would you teach me justice—you—' cried Mrs. Masters, her eyes blazing with anger, 'go to your room and stay there—go——'

Speaking, she turned and gave her daughter a vehement push to emphasise her words. Georgina, fidgeting on one leg, was taken unawares; she tumbled in a heap upon the grass, and though one foot was caught and twisted in the hooped withies that fenced in the graves, she did not move it or even moan. Mrs. Masters and the Rector were terribly frightened. At last she began to groan, complaining of her ankle, her mother, full of pity and remorse, bent over the girl, weeping tears and kisses. She turned to the Rector. 'Go for Dr. Carruthers,' she cried; then bending lower she put her arms tenderly under the girl's shoulder and round her waist. 'Go for the doctor,' she repeated. 'I will carry her into your house until he comes.'

'You !'

But already she had raised the girl, and was carrying her swiftly, staggering, down the side path to the rectory. The Rector stopped a moment, looking after the tall, imperious thin figure, rigid, strained in every nerve, staggering among the tombs. However much he might condemn, the Rector still admired her.

'She is a grand woman,' he muttered, 'a grand woman, but prouder than Lucifer —and she will never forgive that innocent Miss Lawrance.'

CHAPTER VI.

GOOD-BYE !

MEANWHILE Arden, in Venice, lay in a
sort of torpor; never weeping, seldom
speaking, a wan smile mocking the miserable pallor of her face, like wintry sunshine on a grave.

Mrs. Rose was frightened at this
change in the gay, sensitive girl, and
vainly strove to rouse her from her
apathy; but in truth there was nothing
to fear. Arden, whose life had ever been
wrapped round with dreams, was slow to
realise the whole extent of her loss. She
missed her father—he was gone away.
She felt strangely tired and unstrung.
But she could not understand that her

life was changed at once and for ever—that henceforth loneliness, misery, must be her portion.

She lay for hours on the sofa, drowsily watching the gondolas that pass up and down the Canalazzo. As they looked at her, the Roses thought her dying of a broken heart—they scarcely dared to speak to her ; Gerard felt his love a profanation not to be thought of till a happier season. And yet Arden was not really so very unhappy. Numb, inert, lifeless, she often was not thinking of her grief at all, but finding a dreary pleasure in counting the numbers of the boats, or dreaming how she would very soon be dead and with her father, and how sorry they would all be to lose her. Yet she had no clear realisation that her father was gone away for ever—lying dead under the earth. She fancied him bending over her couch, unseen, but near, waiting for her soul, to lead it to the Paradise of Saints.

As the weeks grew on and she became aware that she was not to die just yet, she quickly shuffled another dream between her mind and her misery. She looked upon herself as a messenger sent by her father to console and help his father in his great distress. A year or two spent in unselfish ministry should fit her to die and go to heaven. When her grandfather's letter came, Mrs. Rose handed it to her with a terrible anxiety; it was horrible to tell the child that her future must be spent among strangers. But Arden smiled as she read the letter.

'It is very good of grandpapa,' she said; and lay down again and watched the boats gliding up and down the Canalazzo as before.

'But, my dear, you must do something; you must decide.'

'It is all decided; let me be.'

Mrs. Rose stood irresolute, watching her.

My dear,' she said, 'if it makes you very miserable, don't go. At any rate, don't go yet. We shall be in Europe all this year. Stay with us, my dearie, if you are happier with us.'

' Thank you,' said Arden ; ' how good you are ; but if you only knew how much alike all things are to me now.'

' Oh, stay with us, Arden,' said Gerard, coming forward. And Ellie kissed her more warmly than ever she had done before.

' Papa wished me to go,' she said.

' Well ; perhaps it is best,' said Ellie, her excellent common sense asserting itself again. 'After all, it is more her place than anywhere else.'

They said no more on the subject just then, but often during the next few days Arden would revert, quite without repugnance, to the new life she was to begin.

' I have always been considered by everyone,' she would say ; ' and now I shall consider other people. One can be useful, at least, however dead one's own future seems; and I suppose there is a sort of happiness in being useful. I shall make myself necessary to those kind old people; and the peasants—I shall be good to the peasants in the terrible northern winters.'

No word of regret for Rome; scarcely a pang at parting with her friends. Yet Rome and these friends had been the influencing passions of her childhood.

After two or three days, in which Arden showed herself quite indisposed to do anything more immediate than theorise, Mrs. Rose said to her—

'I think, my child, you should write to your grandfather to-day.'

'Oh yes.'

'And Arden, dear, when you write, you should give him some sort of hint as to when he may expect you.'

'Any time.'

'You would like to go to Rome, first? We are all going at the month's end.'

'Why should I go to Rome?'

'To pack—arrange matters—say good-bye.'

'I am not strong enough; the notary will see to all that.'

Mrs. Rose stared—but only said,

'Oh, I will manage things for you, my darling.'

'Thank you.'

Arden said no more, and took no part in all the arrangements made for her future; her escort was provided, her trunks packed, and she seemed not to understand that she was going away. Sitting there, her head aimlessly drooped at the neck, her hands lying idly in her lap, a wan remembering smile playing round her mouth, no wonder that the two women feared for her reason and Gerard for her life. They scarcely dared to send her away.

But on this point Arden was obstinate.

'I can't be more unhappy than I am,' she said, 'but I'm going to try to be better; I'm going to try to be of use in the world at last.'

She smiled softly; it was her one comfort to think that she would lead a holy life and die young, and soon be at peace. That end should ennoble her short careless years, and be a monument to her father's memory. Henceforth she was dead to the world.

And indeed she made her adieus with something of the solemn apathy to all that is dear and lovely felt by the nun who takes the veil. She was even glad that she must give up all that she cared for—friends, country, companionship, art. For now she was to think not how to live, but how to die.

To the very young it seems so easy to die.

Even when the parting came she was

scarcely moved. A little whiter, a degree more sad, that was all. At the last she clung to Mrs. Rose passionately, closely, as we cling to whatever is dear, proven, familiar, on the brink of the unknown. But the next moment she was calm.

'Good-bye, dear Ellie,' she said, 'don't quite forget me!'

Then Gerard led her a little aside.

'Arden,' he began, 'there's something I want to tell you; something I must— you'll let me come and see you? because now——'

'Now,' said Arden solemnly, 'we can only say good-bye.'

She gave him her hand with a sweet, sad smile, that did not comprehend anything but her own sorrow.

CHAPTER VII.

IN A STRANGE LAND.

THE journey was in truth the best thing
that could have happened to Arden. The
way they went was strange to her; she
could not remember her father by every
turning of the way through France and
Savoy, as in Italy the stones and trees
served to recall him. And the cool air of
the north put fresh spirit into her pros-
trate and weary body. There was a certain
excitement in going so far so fast; these
three days of travel, made with companions
unassociated with other times, had no con-
nection, it seemed, with her past or with
her sorrow. They amused her a little, as
a show at a fair might have done.

Only when they reached London in the

rain, did she realise how great a step she
had taken. She was severed and set apart
from all things familiar and dear. To this
English girl her own country seemed inexpressibly strange; for a long time it was
a surprise to her to hear the common people
talking English. She missed the caressing Roman ways; the pompous meditative
Roman voices ; the soft sunny grey and
deep sapphire blue of Roman skies ; the
very trees she knew the best would not
grow in this strange country. Arden, as
the train whirled her away from London,
away from the travelling-companions who
formed her last link with the South, was
overcome by an unspeakable desolation.
She was so tired, too. She did not want
just now to begin the arduous life of duty
she had so often pictured to herself. She
wanted someone to take care of her. When
she thought of it, how sad it was that just
she, who had always been so loved and
happy, just she should be this friendless

orphan in a strange land. She cried a
little, for sheer pity of herself—poor little
would-be saint of seventeen.

At Arden, itself, there is no station;
but at Raynham, four miles away, there is
a roadside shed, sufficient for the meagre
traffic of the place. Here the train stopped,
and our heroine alighted. It was raining
hard as she stood under shelter, watching
her great trunks and boxes (a marvel to
the solitary porter) being heaped together.
At last they were all out; the man wheeled
them across the line, Arden following sadly
and dismally enough.

She stood looking disconsolately about
her.

'Miss Lawrance?' said the station-
master.

'Yes,' she said. 'Is no one here to
meet me?'

'I'll go and see, Miss.'

The man left her; she sank down on a
bench, half-dead with fatigue.

The man came back after a minute.

'It seems, Miss, being such unkéd weather, Mr. Lawrance thought it best not to send a basket-carriage ; so French the carrier's come to meet you and fetch the boxes in his covered cart.'

'Oh !' said Arden. It all seemed very forlorn—the fatigue, the rain, the discomfort, the lack of welcome. But as yet she would not lose heart.

She went out and stood, her heavy mourning dress all wet and crumpled, watching the two men heap her boxes into the back of the cart. Then they brought her a chair, and she clambered up and seated herself on the broad wooden seat by the side of the carrier. Then the horse started, and jolting, rattling, rumbling, they passed through the lanes.

'It seems very uncomfortable,' thought Arden, 'but perhaps it's the English custom.'

How long the way seemed, through the

lanes bordered with hedges, with always in front the same plan of little irregular fields, with clumps of spongy trees, heavy and lifeless in the thick air ; how very few houses there seemed in the country, and how small they were, those red square ivied buildings, with never a tower or a loggia. But the villages were pretty, and the trees that overhung the lush hedges of the lane.

Tired as she was, Arden's eyes kept glancing up and down, from side to side, eagerly examining the scene of her future.

After they had gone about a mile, the rain cleared off, and the country, fresh and green, smelling of earth and flowers, looked tenfold prettier.

'The sun's come out to welcome you, Miss,' said the carrier, with a broad grin.

'Thank you.'

'Mr. Lawrance was mortal vexed he couldn't ha met you himself, but the long spell of moistish weather's laid him up again with the rheumatics.'

' Oh,' said Arden, ' is he ill? I'm sorry.'

' Lor Miss, he pretty near allus *is* ill ; he's an old man is Mr. Lawrance, and since they sold the 'orse it's seldom he leaves the 'ouse. He's not so strong as he was—not so strong as he was.'

She forgot that she was to be the old man's consoling angel. Poor Arden! How gloomy it all sounded. She wondered if it always rained, if her grandfather was always ill. She remembered that in Rome her dressmaker used to say when it rained—' *Oggi sembra una specie d'Inghilterra.*'

' Does it always rain here ?' she said timidly.

The man looked at her and began to laugh, a sort of suppressed inward chuckle.

' Oh Lor, Miss,' he said, ' you're the very moral of poor Mr. John, so free with his jokes, so affable, as he wor. Does it

allus rain?' he repeated, chuckling to himself, 'and there's the sunshine, as clear as
clear can be.'

At all events it was not on Arden's
face. The fatigue, the gloomy news, the
sight of the pallid watery gleam which she
took for the usual English sun, and most
of all the allusion to her dead father, all
served to overwhelm her with a vague
dismay. She pulled down her veil to hide
the tears in her eyes.

They slackened pace to go up the hill
before Arden church. Her attention was
suddenly aroused by hearing voices in the
lane.

'This is she, I suppose.'

'What a shame to send the carrier's
cart. How like those people!'

'I'm glad they have so much good
sense. Now, mind, Adelaide; no making
friends with her!'

'Hush!'

She looked out. A handsome thin lady

of middle age, a pretty affected-looking girl, with very arched eyebrows and a tiny waist, were walking down the hill.

'Who are they?' said Arden to the carrier.

'It's Mrs. Masters and Miss Masters of the Hall,' he answered, and touched his cap.

'I wonder what they meant,' thought Arden, wondering. Why was the girl told not to make friends with her? They could know nothing about her, good or bad. And when she had reflected a little on this question, she recalled the tone of contempt in which they had spoken of her relations: 'those people.' Evidently they were not considered the equals of those two women, and yet she had been used to have for her friends people at least as refined and considerable. She felt a certain indignation—which was diverted, however, a little towards her own kin, when she reflected that even those rude, haughty passers-by had looked upon it as an insult to fetch her in a carrier's cart. It was all a mystery of painful strangeness, forlornness, anticipated humiliation.

Would the cart never get to its journey's end?

'Are we nearly at the Bushes?' she asked.

'Them two red chimbleys, Miss, over the hill—that's the Bushes. Only ten minutes, and we're there.'

Arden saw the chimneys, but not the hill, and would have wished herself miles away. She could feel her heart beating with anxiety and dread.

They turned a sudden corner, passed a clump of trees, and came to a white gate, to a long neglected drive arched over here and there with apple trees, bordered with overgrown laurels. A few flowers were running to seed in the borders; dandelions, plantains, and chickweed cropped up among the gravel. The man got down and hooked back the gate. Then the cart jogged up the drive.

'Here you are, Miss,' said the man.

And now the house was in view.

A rambling low verandahed house, half modern stucco, half old red brick, all of it clambered over and covered with ivy and roses, clematis and Virginia creepers. The cart dragged heavily through the gravelled drive and stopped at the locked door. The bell was broken, and for a long time they could make no one hear.

It was getting dark and even cold.

'Belike they're all upstairs in the old gentleman's room,' bethought the carrier finally; and he threw some stones up at the window round the corner. Then a light moved—a step crossed the hall— she could hear some one unbolting the door.

'Who's there?' cried someone.

'It's Miss Lawrance,' said the carrier.

Then the door opened, and a pale thin

woman came out, dressed shabbily, even meanly, in a cotton petticoat and jacket.

'It's the housekeeper, I suppose,' thought Arden, and she made no advance.

But the woman came up to her and kissed her.

'Welcome, Arden dear,' she said. 'Come in, child; you must be cold and tired. I've made a fire in the dining room, and kept the dinner late for you. Come, dear, Gay 'll see to your boxes.'

Arden went in. There was a candle in the hall, and she could dimly see the plain and shabby woman who led her in. She could see, as she was led to her room, that the house was shabby too. The handsome carved hall chairs that had been broken long ago remained unmended; the balustrade of the stairs was loose; in her large and pretty bedroom two of the window-sashes were broken.

'You must bolt the door, dear,' said Mrs. Lawrance, 'for we've mislaid the key.'

'I've had a good bright fire made, you see,' went on Mrs. Lawrance, as she helped the tired girl to take off her cloak and hat, 'for grandpa's been so ill aäl day, he can't see you to-night—and I thaät you'd be glad to retire early,' said Mrs. Lawrance.

Arden turned round suddenly, and threw her arms round her.

'How good you are!' she cried. 'I've been so lonely,' and all her dismays and trouble melted in a flood of tears. Ah, now she thought she had found safety and shelter and love ; she had an aim in life again. If the house were dull, if her life would be lonely, welcome and dear should such a life be to her, since love would be with it, love given and received. She would be like a light in the dark, like sun in winter, to her grandfather and his wife ; she would amply repay and over-pay the debt of love she meant to owe them. You see she was still very young and a spoiled child ; little self-reliant, eager

for love and praise, vain, too ; and with so
little of the dramatic power of sympathy
that she could not understand natures and
situations different from her own ; never
guessing that to this elderly devoted couple
the intrusion of a young imperious life into
their cherished quiet was as a light that
dazzles, as a sun that wearies and destroys.
She threw her arms round Mrs. Lawrance's
neck and cried there, sure of being loved
and soothed.

Mrs. Lawrance soothed her, gently,
too, and kindly. But she was alarmed.
What could she do, busy preoccupied
woman that she was, with an hysterical,
fanciful young lady in the house ? All
the time she was speaking softly to Arden,
as one speaks to a crying child, she was
half-unconsciously wishing that her husband's granddaughter had been a stout
able farmer's daughter, taking things
quietly, and exacting and giving little
besides assistance. 'Now I'll leave you,

Arden,' she said. 'I've got to see to the dinner. You'll be easier, most likely child, when you've eaten summat.'

She went out, softly closing the door.

Arden curled herself up on the rug— she leaned her head upon her hand, and looked into the flame. The depression of the journey had suddenly cleared off—her temperament, keenly alive but dreamy, sprang up with a sudden rebound to her old level of light-heartedness.

'I am going to be good and happy,' she said. 'I am going to try and fill papa's place to them, though they cannot fill it to me.'

She imagined all the things she would undertake ; how useful she would be, how English, how unlike anything she ever had imagined. Through all her pleasant visions of self-sacrifice ran a thread of naïve self-congratulation at being able to fill so ably such an unexpected *rôle*.

'If Gerard and Ellie could only know!' she exclaimed once.

And then she forgot her fancies and fell back on memory.

The tears were filling her eyes again, when Mrs. Lawrance tapped at the door and summoned her to dinner.

CHAPTER VIII.

A NEW LIFE.

ARDEN woke up the next morning refreshed and expectant. She got up quickly, and ran downstairs into the sombre old dining-room ; no sign of life there yet ; the clock pointed at half-past six. She heard a clatter in the kitchen, but there she did not venture. So she unlocked the front door and went out into the garden.

Outside it was as pretty as possible, so fresh and bright. The sunbeams glanced off the wet sharp edges of the laurel-leaves ; they looked as bright as spears. All the birds that sing in that season were tuning up. The newly-opened flowers were moist, and fresh, and sweet beyond comparison. Above the green meadows, between the trees, bluish and white mists were still hanging in soft wreaths.

Life, too, in such a moment, seems a bud of uncertain promise; the birds first practising notes before the song, the fragrant misty morning which heralds in the day of storm and the day of ripening sun alike.

That morning the freshness and strangeness of things had driven Arden's sorrow out of sight for an hour, as there comes sometimes a lull in sharp pain, during which the pillows are softer, the air sweeter, the view out of the window more full of meaning and colour than ever it was before. Something of this renewed delight in life had fallen for a moment to Arden's lot. She walked down the lane, her head thrown back, singing very softly; the fresh keen air struck a colour up her cheeks. In her black clothes she looked very young, and delicate, and fresh; like a spring day before the trees begin to bud. She did not hear a sound to tell of anyone near at hand, or she would have stopped her singing; she did not see anyone, or she would not have flourished the long sprays of honeysuckle she had gathered in the hedge. Yet she was seen and overheard; and to one person the thought of her was always coloured by that first impression; to one person she would henceforth remain a creature of frail, unearthly loveliness, crowned with golden hair, with a face like a blossom, a voice that was a song, a step springing with youth and grace, her hands full of flowers, her eyes full of light, yet clad in heavy, deep, black mourning; a creature to be loved but not to love, herself impervious to all earnest passion; only clothed with loss and misery and sorrow and love foregone, not changed through and through by the experience of these things.

Meanwhile Arden, unaware what im-

pressions of her were taking shape, went
singing down the lane, while on the other
side the hedge Farmer Williams forgot his
fields of corn in looking after that golden
head. But Arden did not know, and had
she known would have paid no heed. She
went down the lane till it turns sharply
below the canal-bridge, and there suddenly
a choking in her throat, a mist in her eyes,
a pang in her very heart, took away again
her short-lived gladness.

'You don't know what it's like, Arden;
those green villages, the red little thatched
houses nestling under great oaks and elms;
the green where the geese feed and the
boys play cricket, with a pond at one end
for the ducks; the village inn with its
great swinging sign—I often think I
should like to see it again.'

She seemed to hear her father's voice
distinctly repeating the words she so well
remembered, but she would never, never
feel again the loving pressure of the arm

that held her when she heard them. Her father was dead. The thought struck Arden with a terrible shock, familiar as it was. Dead! She could not cry; she seemed deafened, dumb, bruised, lifeless; she sank on a large stone under a tree, and let the cruel memories surge in upon her wave on wave. If her father had come to Arden he would not have died. Oh, it was terrible; there was something worse behind, among these fearful cloudy thoughts—she would not think it. She rose wildly from her seat and began walking homewards quickly, almost running, with a vague childish purpose of leaving her troubles behind her, like a dropped burden, by the white stone on the village green.

She soon reached home, and found the breakfast-table spread and her grandfather waiting for her in the big leathern chair by the hearth. There was sufficient likeness to her father in the kindly indolent

old face to make Arden's eyes fill with
sudden tears. There were sufficient traces
of his son in Arden's slight, tall figure and
delicate air to make her grandfather sharply
realise that this was no stranger he had
taken to his hearth, but a living reminder
of forgotten losses long supplanted, a
keeping open of old wounds, a survival of
a past which he had chosen long ago to
bury out of sight.

For a moment he thought of that past
with renewed tenderness, talking to Arden
of her father, his son. They spoke of old
times. The hours glided by, and Arden
almost felt she possessed her happiness
again, recalling it thus. As the sun grew
high, they left the house and sat talking,
like old friends, in the cool verandah.
Mr. Lawrance, roused to more interest
than he had shown for years, heard the
history of his son's life, of his pictures, and
their success ; of his home, of his death-
bed ; and he, in his turn, told Arden about

her father's youth, about her mother, what they had all said and done together in this very house where she had come to live, under this very verandah where she was sitting.

Indeed, a passer-by would have thought it a typical scene of home life—the old man, the young girl talking together earnestly ; Mrs. Lawrance, with her great basket of needlework, sewing busily a little apart.

Only, if she had lifted her eyes from her work, one would have seen an ominous pale gleam in them ; have noticed how the lips were pressed into a thin white line, how her cheeks burned as she looked on, unheeded, while this young girl, this stranger who had never nursed him, filled her husband's mind, filled it to the brim with recollections of a time, a life, in which she had no past, which was her enemy, which would have disowned her, cast her out.

Meanwhile, quite unconsciously Arden and Mr. Lawrance went on talking.

'And did John really ever speak of coming to see me? Poor fellow, poor fellow——'

'Oh, yes; he used to speak of the village; say he should like to see it again, and, grandpapa, he always used to say that you would keep a home and a welcome for me.'

'Ay, ay; he might well be sure of that; we've always got a welcome here for those who want us. Haven't we, Annie?'

Mrs. Lawrance did not answer, but her silence passed unnoticed.

'I wish he had come, John. I suppose he got to look quite an elderly man?'

'Oh, no; no one was ever so handsome as papa; none of the people in Rome.'

'Ay, he was a handsome lad, more like his mother than like me. She was so proud of him. Ah, well!'

The old man sighed.   Arden drew her chair closer.

'I think you are like him, too, grand-papa.'

'Ah, child, it's a sad thing to live out all one's interests ; but, there, have you got a likeness of John ?'

'Of papa ? see here.'

She unclasped a locket thrust into her dress, revealing a handsome, refined, in-dolent face.   She showed it to her grand-father.

'He was so good,' she sobbed out.

'Poor fellow ; poor John!   And he was getting on so well, you say ?'   He took the little locket, and looked at it silently for some minutes.   Mrs. Lawrance got up hurriedly and came towards them, as if to look too.   Suddenly she dashed the locket out of the old man's hand on to the gravel.

'He was a bad son,' she cried ; 'a cruel son !'

Arden started to her feet.

'For shame! How dare you, how dare you? Grandpapa!'

She came up to him pale, aghast, holding the arm of his chair.

'She doesn't mean it, child,' cried Mr. Lawrance. 'Annie, tell the child at once that you didn't mean to hurt her.'

Mrs. Lawrance stood quite still, impassive to all appearance; but a tumult of pride, remorse, hatred, and jealousy was raging in her heart. She said nothing, but continued looking at the most distant fields.

'Do you hear?' said Mr. Lawrance, sternly.

'After aäl, I am your wife!' she said.

'Yes, yes,' said Mr. Lawrance testily, 'of course you are. And I never regretted it till now. It's your own fault, Annie, if I'm angry with you, and it is ungrateful, and unwomanly, and unwifely in you.'

'Ah!' she gasped. 'I'm sorry.'

'There, there,' went on the old gentleman, discomfited by his wife's bitter smile
and Arden's frightened face, 'that's right,
Annie. We're friends again now, friends
again now.'

'I'm sorry to have ever grieved you,'
interrupted his wife; 'it is not your faält.
It is her's; that child's. She is taking my
life away with her memories and her interests! But there; you'd better go, child.
I don't want to hurt you.'

'There, there, be quiet, Annie,' cried
poor perplexed Mr. Lawrance. 'Perhaps
you'd better do as she says, Arden, child.
She's overstrained, hysterical. She's not
very well, I think. She doesn't mean you
any harm, but perhaps you'd better begin
your unpacking.'

He turned towards his wife, who had
sunk back on the bench. Arden turned
away. So this was the beginning of her
mission !

She went into her own room, and sat

down on one of the ranged unopened
boxes. She felt, strange to say, more
wounded by her grandfather's calm dis-
missal than by Mrs. Lawrance's bitter
words. Anger, at least, is not indifference;
and to her grandfather she had been consciously affectionate—and he had dismissed
her.

She had been used to a different return
for her affection, for she had been all her
life a spoilt child, loved and worshipped.
How surprised, she thought, they would
be, those old people, could they know how
she had been cared for in Rome. Then
softer feelings came; she resolved to think
no more of herself; she would be loving,
and helpful, and necessary to them,
despite their hardness.

At last she heard a knock at the
door.

She started; she wanted to tell the
person outside to enter; it added a new
force to her sense of the strangeness and

newness of everything, that she really did not know how to say it in English ; never having spoken English, save in conversation with her equals, in all her life.

' Forwards ! ' ventured Arden.

The knock was repeated. Arden, despite her forlornness, began to laugh. She went to the door herself and opened it ; the little servant stood outside.

' Please, miss,' she said, ' master says this, will you come down to tea, miss, or will you have it sent upstairs ? '

' Oh, come, I'm not a punished child. Say I'll be down in a minute.'

She walked downstairs with a very stately air.

' I'm glad to see you're so sensible, Sylvia,' said her grandfather. ' Come and get your supper, there's a good girl.'

' Sylvia ! ' she stared at him with widening eyes

Mr. Lawrance looked at his wife ; she said nothing.

'It seems, my dear,' he began, a little disconcerted; 'it seems, my dear, Arden—Sylvia, I mean—the rector has told us this afternoon that Mrs. Masters of the Hall is very much affronted at your bearing her family name; she's a quick-tempered woman, but she's the principal person of the place; and it's as well, my dear, coming into a new place, that you should make friends with—with——'

'The Mammon of unrighteousness,' finished Mrs. Lawrance, concluding the quotation with perfect gravity.

Arden began to laugh. 'Poor Mrs. Masters!' she said.

Mrs. Lawrance looked inexpressibly shocked; but she said nothing. The old gentleman explained:—

'My wife doesn't like to hear the Bible laughed at, Arden,' he said in the tone of an *esprit fort*, not himself outraged, but careful of the sensibilities of tenderer spirits.

'I beg your pardon,' said Arden, with a quaint little foreign bow ; then, turning to her grandfather, 'And so Mrs. Masters doesn't like my name ?'

'No, no, she's a queer-tempered woman ; it seems she knocked down Miss Georgina and half-broke her ankle because the child said she'd like to know you.'

'What a charming acquaintance!'

'Well ; she's a woman of very good birth, the last of the Ardens of Arden. She's a right to be proud.'

'Pride is a mortal sin,' said Mrs. Lawrance.

'Especially when it breaks one's children's bones,' added Arden.

'Well, well ; don't let us judge our neighbours,' said the old man. 'Judge not, you know, that ye be not judged. I'm not one for being hard on people's frailties.'

'That you're not, dear,' said his wife, and, with a new sweeter look on her face, and a smile that included even Arden, she said, 'You've got a good grandfather, Sylvia; you may thank God for that!'

Arden, a little impatient of this devotion, turned to her grandfather—

'And am I to change my name to please a woman I never heard of?' she asked a little sharply.

'Sylvia's a pretty name,' replied Mr. Lawrance. 'And to call you "Arden," here, has about as much sense or meaning as to call you "Parish Church."'

'Besides, it's your own name, you know, Sylvia; we don't choose it out for you,' added Mrs. Lawrance.

'True,' said the girl. 'Call me Sylvia then; Arden was quite a different person.'

'That's right,' cried Mr. Lawrance, glad to be rid of the discussion.

But his wife's heart failed her a little (for she was very tender to visible suffering) at sight of the girl's whitened face.

'Don't take it so to heart, dearie,' she said.

'Oh, no ; I don't take it to heart,' answered Arden. 'Better the new name with the new life.'

CHAPTER IX.

AN ENGLISH SUNDAY.

MEANWHILE that very evening a more comfortable supper-party—also of three persons—was chatting, eating, and drinking at the next house down the lane. There was no prettier room in Arden than the Williams's big, brown wainscotted parlour. You went down two oak steps into it, and the three square windows were on a level with the stocks and gillyflowers and gay striped roses of the flower garden outside. At the other a staircase, also of oak, led to the upper storey. The room itself was wainscotted nearly to the ceiling, where a broad oaken beam supported the plaster ; and at the door-ward side of the huge,

overhanging chimney, a broad oak settle,
high in the back, fenced off all danger
of draught. Under the windows there
was a heavy old chest like a Florentine
cassone, cushioned at the top for a seat,
while if you lifted up the lid, piles of
white lavender-scented table-linen revealed
its second purpose. It was pleasant in
summer days to sit on the red cushion
with the flowers waving through the
window on a level with one's face. Over
head hung a canary cage, and on either
side of the chest, a sewing machine on a
stand and a little work-table told that
the parlour was a woman's sitting-room.
There was also set beside an oaken linen-
press, a little curly velvet sofa placed so
as to secure the light from the windows
and the warmth from the fire. The tall
upright clock was faced by a cottage
piano with Handel's ' Messiah ' open on the
ledge ; the old bureau had its glazen-faced
shelves well-filled with books ; and a

volume of ' Poésies choisies,' some French school books and prizes, an odd number of Michelet's ' History of France,' Carlyle on ' Hero-worship,' and ' The Mill on the Floss,' stood shoulder to shoulder there with the ' Guide to Farriery,' some books on farming, and the Family Bible. This contrast between the hereditary possessions of the family and the tastes of its present members, gave a pleasant character and homeliness to the parlour.

Although it was summer-time, a little gaily-blazing fire lit up the depths of the chimney, and made pleasant lights and shadows on the crimson hangings. It flickered, mingling with the dim light of the fading day, on the faces of two women and a man, who, having finished supper, still lingered at the table talking. By the uncertain light you would have called Harry Williams an ugly man, for he was square, short, and heavily-built, with a thick neck and large head; his handsome frank blue eyes, his firm and smiling mouth and ruddy skin were all in shadow ; but such was the magic of his pleasant smile that by daylight you would have thought him a likely fellow. The woman facing him, his step-mother, belonged to an opposite type. A draper's clever daughter, 'finished' at a cheap convent-school in Belgium, she had essayed semi-gentility as a nursery-governess; but her health broke down while she was teaching the children of a former Rector of Arden, and then Harry's father, chief farmer and organist of the parish, had asked her, for the third time, to marry him. This time she accepted him as a *pis-aller*, and her decision made Edward Williams very happy. He was of a weaker nature than his son, more of a seeker after ideals, and to him the Vicar's pretty governess appeared a creature indefinably rare, refined, and elevated. She brought her second-rate accomplishments, her cheap piano and French convent prizes, to make the Paradise her husband looked for. He did not find it in his love, this ideal existence; then he went to the alehouse, and certainly he did not find it there. Harry, a lad of fourteen, set to work to stop this madness, and his force of will and patient love were strong enough to save his father from the habitual degradation of an unconquered evil habit.

Mrs. Williams made no difficulty about accepting his penitence: she did not look for ideals, and flourished well enough in the plenteous well-to-do existence of her married life, without asking or giving a great degree of affection, and generally acting upon the principle of letting well and ill alike alone. During this St. Martin's summer of peace and domestic comfort, ten years after their marriage, Susie was born. The baby did even more than the imperious Harry in keeping her father from the alehouse; but the man's health was already ruined. One wet spring an epidemic of typhus devastated the village ; Farmer Williams was among the first to die. Harry then was left the master of a farm, deteriorated by long mismanagement, the only protector of a sickly, incapable step-mother, and a child of eight years old.

As Susie grew older she strengthened his hands ; of a subtler, more eager, more enthusiastic character than her brother, she possessed much of his energy, decision, and practical activity. She had a mind that grew in all directions like a well-rounded tree ; from her mother she learned all the mother had to give, taking the means from her and turning them to other ends. She learned to play, and discarded Sydney Smith for Handel ; learned French, and laid aside the ' Poésies choisies,' for an odd volume of Michelet's ' History of France,' that had been given her by a visitor at the Rectory, interested in the quaint little girl who played the organ at the

week-day practices. This book, then some
volume of Carlyle, bought with hardly-
kept savings ; then a novel of George
Eliot's—these had been the events of one
side of her life. Equally important, in
another way, was the gradual reform of
the dairy management, the saving and
superiority of the housekeeping since, at
fifteen, the intrepid little Susie had taken
it upon her shoulders. The brother and
sister went together like two good horses
in harness, with an equal pace to one end :
the ameliorating of their inherited condition. The mother, with facile stand-aloof
affection, looked on idly, did not comprehend, but applauded.

All in all, it was a close-knit and happy
family circle.

They were talking together this evening, talking of Arden of course.

' Poor girl,' cried Mrs. Williams, sigh-
ing, ' to be condemned to Arden after the
gay world ! '

'She didn't seem to pine this morning,' said her step-son, rather grimly.

'I daresay ; she doesn't know what it means yet, a country life, an English country life !'

Mrs. Williams sighed again, feeling her superiority in experience.

'If she's a good girl, she'll find plenty to do at the Bushes,' said Susie ; 'they've sadly mismanaged things, those two old people. The carrier says he nearly always brings half their butter back unsold ; and we—we can't make half enough.'

'Ah, you can't expect every girl to be as clever as Susie,' cried Mrs. Williams, 'and such a student, too !'

'She's, maybe, better at book-learning than at dairy-work—Lawrance's maid,' said Harry. 'The parson tells me she's lived all her loife in Rome, among artists and such-like,—her father was an artist.'

'In Rome !' Susie's eyes blazed with historic memories and wonder.

'Is she a Catholic?' asked Mrs. Williams.

'I doant know. We shall see o' Sundays. Folk 'll look more at her than at their neighbours' bonnets to-morrow.'

'You shouldn't speak so Warwickshire, Harry. I declare I'm quite ashamed of you!' exclaimed Mrs. Williams.

'Why shouldn't I speak Warwickshire? It 'ud be odd if I spoke different; the Williamses have lived in this house and farmed Warwickshire land for over two centuries. I'm too proud to think shame o' them and my county.'

'And what will the like of this Miss Lawrance think of you? She'll fancy you're no better than a farm-servant.'

'Oh, mother, we shan't be troubled with Miss Lawrance's opinions. We're not gentlefolk!' cried Susie, a little bitterly.

'At any rate your mother's no mere housekeeper, like Mrs. Lawrance.' This was true, and in so different a sense from that which Mrs. Williams had intended, that there was no help for laughing. All three joined in a peal of good-natured hilarity.

' Dear little mother ! ' cried Susie, cocking her head on one side to observe more critically the slender and faded prettiness of her mother.

' Ay, she wasn't made for dairy work,' joined in Harry ; who had the odd sort of delight in his step-mother's incapability that able men often find in peculiarly helpless women.

' Miss Lawrance is just such a nesh one, I should think ! ' he exclaimed.

' Well, that settles the question *pro tem.* ! ' cried Susie, ' and now I must get to my work. Mother, how am I to translate : " Liège allait faire rendre gorge aux procureurs de l'évêché ?" '

Mrs. Williams' withered French was not equal to the demand, and as usual Susie had recourse to the dictionary, without the

least diminution in her reliance on her
mother's attainments. For a good hour she
was lost in translating, with the difficulty
of a self-taught person, with the lack of
spontaneity of one who reads in a dead
language, Michelet's account of the sack
of Dinant. She was determined to pass
the Cambridge examination, to take her
certificate ; and some time, when Harry
was married, when there would be no more
need or place for her at home, she would
go and teach, she would go and learn, would
live with cultivated people, travel perhaps ;
she would earn and save, and set up an
efficient school for girls ; and her mother
should come and live with her ; thus she
would pass a useful noble life. These were
Susie's long-loved dreams, though of late
they had not quite satisfied her, and had
seemed to lose their savour. Meanwhile
her brother made up his accounts, and Mrs.
Williams lay on the sofa and talked, hum-
ming softly to herself, with characteristic

disregard of the occupations of busier
people. So the evening passed and brought
the night; and the night—welcome to early-
rising country people—the night passed also
and brought the most eventful day of the
week, Sunday.

A country Sunday in summer, an English country Sunday; the fields are still,
no figures move, no voices are heard among
the waving ranks of the ripening corn;
only placid animals populate the pasture
lands still vivid with the green of aftermath; the movement, the voices of the
work-a-day world are stilled. Over all is
an unusual repose. Repose, but not silence.

There are no carts in the fields, no
working reapers and gleaners; but see on
the road, family by family, at unequal intervals, all alike, rich and poor, saunter
along the same way. There are no voices
in the fields, but over the twitter of the
children picking flowers in the hedge-rows,
over the sedater talk of the mothers and

fathers walking on before, over the song of
the birds and the lowing of the cattle, a
sound, a clang, a peal of bells announces
the holiday.

Arden woke up on Sunday morning
refreshed, expectant. She came downstairs
with a bright winning face.

'Good morning, Sylvie,' said Mrs
Lawrance.

'Good morning. How is grandpapa ?'

'He's better this morning. I'll make a
shift to take you to church, as it's the first
time.'

'That's very good of you. I do want
to see all the people, and to hear who they
are.'

'Don't talk at random, child. If you
go to church with such thoughts as that, it
'ull do you no good. No good 'ull come of
it !'

'True.' Arden wondered what she
should say next.

'Who is the clergyman; do you like him?' she asked.

'Mr. Law? He's a good sort of man and a great scholard, so they say; but he don't see after the parish much; he's so taken up with his books and with them Masters.'

'Oh! I shall see Mrs. Masters.' Arden thought of the words she had overheard on the Church Hill, and of Mrs. Masters' request that the name of Arden should be discarded.

'She must be an insolent woman,' she reflected aloud.

'Oh, Sylvie, learn a little respect. You shouldn't speak so of your betters.'

'I don't see that Mrs. Masters is my better, Mrs. Lawrance.'

'She's the Squire's lady, and an Arden of Arden.'

'And I'm an Arden of Rome—a yet more illustrious birthplace.'

'Oh, well, Sylvie, if you choose to

take it ill, you must. But put on your
things, or we'll be late for church ; it's a
longish walk, even across the fields.'

The first bell was just beginning its
clear, far-resounding peal as they left the
house. Arden walked quickly.

'There's no occasion to be so precipi-
tate, Sylvie,' said Mrs. Lawrance ; 'there's
a good half-hour yet, afore service-time.'

'Very well. What lovely roses'—she
stopped, and sniffed the fragrance of a
yellow-sprinkled standard.

'Yes, they're a remarkable fine blossom. Glory-die-Johns, as I've 'eard.'

'What ?'

'That's their botanic name, Glory-die-
John.'

'Oh, how funny, how absurd !' Arden
began to laugh.

'Why, Sylvie, I should ha' thart you'd
ha' known it a'ready ; it's a French word,
so I'm told.'

'True.' Arden buried her blushing

face in the roses, and felt she should not
have laughed.

They walked on a little way in silence.
'I must make another start,' thought
Arden.

'Who lives in that beautiful old house?'
she inquired. 'Oh, what a beautiful black
and white house; it's the first really English house I have ever seen!'

'That's Williams's Farm,' said Mrs.
Lawrance. 'There's nought as I can see
so remarkable about it. Why, Sylvie, the
Bushes is a much better 'ouse than that!'

'But this,' cried the young girl, 'is
so individual; *voila du caractère*, as Gerard
would say. Oh, I should like to paint it.'

'And who's Gerard, Sylvie?' asked
Mrs. Lawrance, with a sudden interest.

'Oh, he's my oldest friend, he and
Ellie. He's a dear boy!' said Arden.

'Oh,' cried Mrs. Lawrance, 'I thart he
might ha' been summat else.'

Arden shook her head, but she did not

laugh, as she would have done a month ago when Gerard was only a nice lad and a dear friend. Now he represented much more ; home, country, her old life, her accustomed thoughts, youth, happiness, art. It was a pity Gerard Rose had no good fairy to whisper that his hour had arrived ; for I think she would have married him then, without being at all in love—not even enough to know that her heart was free.

All this time she was leaning over the rickyard-gate, and Susie Williams, putting on her bonnet, upstairs, could see her well. 'How sweet she looks,' thought Susie. 'How lovely she is in that plain black dress, and long black veil. She looks like the nuns at Clinton. If only she would once look up and smile.'

But Arden moved away.

'Come, Sylvie,' cried Mrs. Lawrance ; 'I should ha' thart you'd ha' seen a farm before, even in furrin parts.'

' Oh, Italian farms are quite different.'

' Ay, I daresay they're not so well kep'. Susie Williams is a good 'un to manage.'

' Is she the farmer's wife ? '

' No ; she's 'is step-sister, and quite a girl ; 'e's never married, 'asn't Williams. So you don't have farms in Rome, Sylvie?'

' Not in Rome, of course, but in the country. Oh, in Tuscany there are such pretty farms ; quite small, you know ; up a hill, with no hedges, and with olive-yards instead of apple-orchards, and under-neath the olives, wheat or maize. You can't think how pretty it is in August, when they hang the maize to dry; it looks like a cloth of gold on the house-fronts, with square holes left for the windows and the door ; and later on you see them ploughing under the olives, with great white oxen, yoked to the plough—not an iron plough, you know, but a sort of wooden trident ; and in the spring the

corn comes up all full of blood-red tulips ;
and round the edges of the fields are pollard mulberry-trees, and the vine jumps
along from tree to tree.'

'Here's the last stile, Sylvie. Ah, we
must show you an English farm ; we're
much more advanced in ageracultur, here.'

And now in front of them rose the
squat grey church, and the high graveyard full of early-coming worshippers.

It was the custom at Arden for all the
farmers of the parish, and their families,
to come to church a good twenty minutes
or so before service-time. In the pretty
high-lying churchyard, they stood in knots
discussing the weather and the prospects
of the harvest; such as were old, or weak,
or tired, sat themselves, with no irreverent
thoughts, on the square box-like tombs.
It was a rendezvous, looked forward to
all the week, where all ends of the parish
met at one centre. Here the elderly
women gossiped together over their neigh-

bours, their housekeeping, and their ail-
ments ; the young people found this their
best chance for meeting friends from distant farms, and for showing themselves off
in their prettiest clothes to their sweet-
hearts. Often, in the muddy, short winter
days, Farmer King's Milly, at Feversham,
for instance, would have found it quite
impossible to tell her secrets to her bosom
friend, Annie Lovell, of Raynham, since
their houses were five miles apart, had
it not been for the pleasant Sunday
mornings when friends met, lovers whispered, merry girls and boys carried on
noisy quarrels and flirtations ; and the
elder people, too, amused themselves in
their own fashion. Of course, the gentry,
having leisure, carriages, a score of means
for meeting in the week, did not avail
themselves of this opportunity. The
Masters, old Mr. Lucy, of Raynham,
Mrs. Clinton, of the Firs (Mrs. Masters'
aunt), and the Lawrances—this was all

the list of gentry—showed their superiority by coming later, when all the
humbler worshippers were seated in their
pews ; the Masters, in especial, often kept
the congregation in the church, and the
clergyman in the vestry, for a good five
minutes ; but no one would have thought
of beginning service without the family
from the Hall.

There was, therefore, quite an as-
semblage of lookers-on to greet Arden's
appearance at church with Mrs. Lawrance.
All turned their heads to gaze at the
two women, with a broad agricultural
stare, innocent of rudeness.

'She's none so pretty, after all; as
white as a potato.'

'Poor maid, she's lost her father.'

'She's a goodly height; 'ud be a fine
figure of a woman if she was filled out
and rosy.'

'Oh, she'll allus be weak and sickly,
take my word.'

' 'Tis a good thing for the Bushes; them two old 'uns let all run to rack and ruin.'

' She's no good, she's a furriner; don't know cheese from chalk.'

' She's welcome as flowers in May, depend upon it.'

The last speaker was Susie Williams, who, having perceived that Arden must have heard too many of the foregoing remarks, made hers in a clear, reassuring voice.   Arden heard her, and smiled. ' Who is that fair-haired, eager-looking girl?' she asked of Mrs. Lawrance.

' That's Miss Williams. Good morning, Miss Williams, I hope your mother's less precarious in 'ealth than formerly.'

' Yes, thank you, Mrs. Lawrance; she's all right.'

Then Arden and Mrs. Lawrance went down into the church, a cold and gloomy barn of a place, lower than the churchyard.

' What a nice girl she seems,' said Arden.

' H-sh. Don't talk in church.'

So Arden set herself to watch her neighbours and to remark the service; she had scarcely ever been to an English service before. In Rome she and her father nearly always went into the country on Sundays; and Arden was not of a religious temperament. She went to church if other people went; of her own accord, she would probably have stayed outside.

The Lawrances' pew was half-way up the aisle; a great square wooden pew, a pillar blocking up one end, the door the other; Mrs. Lawrance sat facing the altar; Arden facing the door; she looked curiously about. On the other side the aisle the bell-ringers were still pulling at the strong many-coloured cords, stooping and rising, dragged off their feet sometimes by the upward jerk of the rope. Down the aisle marched the school children, with fat rosy cheeks drawn into an expression of decent composure, their little eyes cast down,

their whitish or dead-brown hair oiled to
unnatural and dripping glossiness. Then
the old men came in, one by one, and
hobbled to their places in the free seats;
old men with bent shoulders, wrinkled
faces burnt a fine red with exposure to all
weathers, with snowy clean hair, with an
expression of shrewdness and content in
their rugged but not unhandsome outlines.
They sat three rows deep at the top corner
of the aisle; the sun from the window
behind brought out the strong colouring
of their faces and neck-ties, the golden-
brown tints of their fustian jackets.

'They are as superior to the old men
in Rome as their children are expression-
less and ugly,' thought Arden. 'How I
wish Mrs. Lawrance did not look so severe.
I should like to sketch that head!'

She was saved from yielding to the
temptation by a renewed curiosity as a
third inroad from the churchyard crowded
the aisle. Decent labourers and their

wives, some of the farmers, too, with their
families. The bell-ringers stopped ; gradually the church filled. Arden noticed Susie
Williams passing to her seat; the two girls
looked at each other and smiled.

'I should like to know her,' whispered
Arden to Mrs. Lawrance.

'I don't know as she's a proper
acquaintance for you.'

' Not proper?'

' Oh, she's a good girl enough, but
her brother's a coarse man, quite the
farmer.'

By 'coarse,' Mrs. Lawrance meant
rough. But Arden understood her differently.

' Oh,' she said, ' what a pity ! '

There was a pause. After a minute
or two, a rustling. Enter a tall handsome
woman in a shabby silk dress, several girls,
two young men. One of the girls limped
a little, and leaned heavily on the arm of
her brother, a weak, handsome youth.

'Them's the Masters,' said Mrs. Lawrance.

Then service began.

It seemed very long and dull to Arden, the singing bad, the ceremonial dreary, but the waving of the trees outside the window was pretty to watch ; the people, too, seemed far more in sober earnest over their prayers than the worshippers at grand Roman functions. How they listened to the pompous, scholarly sermon ! Arden found her thoughts running back to the near, vanished past ; a heavy tear dropped on to her knee. She shook her head and looked up ; someone was looking at her, earnestly and kindly. She noticed that he was sitting next to Susie Williams.

'So that's the coarse brother, I suppose. What an ugly man ! What insolence to stare at me !'

Her expression conveyed her thoughts; the man looked confused, opened his prayer-book, began reading the Psalms at random.

' I wonder when the Roses will write to me,' Arden was thinking.

After a while the sermon came to an end: the service also. There was a bustle, a general scuffle after umbrellas and prayer-books, an exodus. Arden found herself in the churchyard again, in the fresh clear weather, among the grass and the trees ; she stood still on the path. Mrs. Lawrance nudged her. ' Stand aside, let Mrs. Masters pass.'

She moved a little on to the grass. It was just about the place where Georgina Masters had fallen and hurt her ankle ; the girl was pointing it out to her brother as she passed. ' I think mother's very unjust,' she added.

Mrs. Masters heard ; she turned sharp round.

' Mrs. Lawrance, I haven't seen you for an age,' she said ; ' and how's your husband, pray ?'

Mrs. Lawrance was delighted at this

mark of recognition, though she was too proud to show it.

'Mr. Lawrance is allus a sufferer,' she said, 'and 'e's just lost 'is only son, a circumstance as has proved very injurious to 'is 'ealth ; but 'e'll be pleased to 'ear you was so kindly interested'—Mrs. Lawrance hesitated a moment, then she pushed Arden forward—'Mr. Lawrance's granddaughter is come to live with us,' she said.

'Oh, mother!' cried Georgina, coming forward.

Mrs. Masters put up her eyeglass, and looked at Arden.

'Is this the young person? I have not the pleasure of her acquaintance.'

Then she swept onwards, with one triumphant glance at Georgina ; swept on, leaving behind her a confused murmur of reproaches, gossip, wonder, from the stragglers in the churchyard.

'For shame ; the insolent woman!' cried Susie Williams.

Arden stepped forward. 'Thank you!' she said, and held out her hand.

'Come on, Sylvie, come on,' cried Mrs. Lawrance, 'we've had quite enough commotion for one Sunday a'ready.'

Arden obeyed; but that warm friendly hand-clasp remained in her memory, a full equivalent for Mrs. Masters' injury.

'Brother or no brother, I will know that girl,' she said to herself, 'especially as it seems I am to be allowed to know nobody else.'

CHAPTER X.

THE PRIMROSE PATH.

THAT afternoon, as Susie Williams and her mother were returning from some neighbourly visit, they met the Squire's youngest son in the lane. This was such an important event to little Susie, and summoned such blushes to her cheeks, that we must not pass over in silence a young man whose merits certainly deserve no chronicle.

Fred Masters was the darling of his mother and sisters; they had always spoiled him from affection, as his father had done from vanity, for Fred was the very reproduction of his own extravagant indolent youth. The lad was now about

twenty-three years of age, a very handsome, youthful, petulant, engaging scapegrace. In the spring he had been suddenly
expelled from Cambridge for some over-
daring undergraduate's 'lark,' but though
this escapade was the nominal cause of his
being sent down, people talked of worse
unsteadiness behind. Since then he had
loitered about the village, doing nothing,
making friends with all the village wits,
sworn admirers of this handsome youth,
who treated them all round at the Three
Crowns ; and of late he had found a still
more pleasing pastime in making love to
pretty Susie Williams.

So far his love-making had never gone
any great lengths. There was a certain
dignity in Susie's frank recognition of her
inferior station, a certain impregnability in
her ardent earnestness in all she did, which
warned the idle youth against checkmating
all pleasant possibilities by proceeding to
extremes. All he could do was to infuse

much chivalry and devotion into his manner at choir practices, and at the Sunday school, at which Susie's presence had made him a regular attendant. This promising youth was strolling down the lane when he saw Susie Williams and her mother a little ahead.

'Plague take the little old woman,' he said to himself, 'she is always in the way.'

However, when he came up to them, he took off his hat, and made himself even more agreeable to Mrs. Williams than to the daughter.

'I missed you at church this morning, Mrs. Williams. I hope you did not stay at home from illness?'

'Oh, Mr. Fred, you're always so polite and noticing. No, I'm quite well, I am thankful to say; but there's a mint of things to do about the house, and Susie's so fond of her church and school.'

'So am I.' Fred tried to look meaningly at Susie, but she did not understand.

'One ought to love institutions,' she replied.

'Certainly she is very stupid sometimes,' reflected the young man.

'Oh, yes, Mr. Fred,' went on Mrs. Williams, 'everyone knows you're the stay of the school; the Vicar's so lost in his book-learning. This last six months or so, Susie tells me, you've been so constant in looking after things and helping her manage that class of great unruly boys that I always say she is unfit to look after.'

Fred smiled a little awkwardly, and changed the topic.

'Are you going to church this evening, Miss Susie? There's to be a practice after service, so Georgina tells me.'

'I wish I could come, but it's so late getting home.'

'Let her come, Mrs. Williams. I'll see her home, if you think I'm a fit escort.'

'Oh, Mr. Fred!' cried the honoured and delighted Mrs. Williams.

'I think I can't come,' cried Susie, feeling tremendously willing and unwilling, shy and eager, all at once. 'In fact, I am sure I can't come. Harry wants me.'

'I wish you would come, Miss Susie '— this low to her; then louder to her mother, 'The Vicar always complains when she is absent. She is the one contralto of the village : I think Mr. Williams might spare her.'

'Never fear, Mr. Fred. She'll come— there's nothing she wants so much.'

'Mother !' cried Susie, in an appealing voice.

'I shall see you then,' said the young man. 'I am glad. Good-bye, Mrs. Williams.'

Fred sauntered on: it was not so easy after all; yet he was from lack of anything else to think of becoming desperately in love with this yellow-haired little girl.

Mrs. Williams and her daughter went slowly on in the opposite direction.

'Why did you insist on my going this evening, mother? You know I promised to look over the accounts with Harry.'

'Don't speak so sharp, Susie. I shouldn't have insisted unless it were for your good. And I wish you'd call me "mama," not "mother." 'Tis more ladylike.'

'I don't care ; I am not a young lady.'

'Oh, Susie, Susie, don't say such things ; people take one at one's own value ; and there's no knowing what may happen.'

'After all,' sighed Susie, 'it is no great matter, I suppose, if I am a good woman.'

She sighed ; because she could not help thinking how nice it would have been had she been born a young lady ; she would have known Mr. Fred's sisters.

'We shall see,' said Mrs. Williams. She smiled to herself ; now if the Squire's younger son, none too well off, should marry her Susie, who was as pretty a girl as one could wish to see and would have a thousand pounds to her portion, why it would be an excellent thing for him, and she would live to see her daughter a real lady. Her fancy ran far ahead; it was all settled in her mind, when Susie's voice brought her back to reality:

'Miss Lawrance is a young lady,' she was saying, 'and such a beautiful young lady! Yet she doesn't look happy; she's not so happy as I, poor girl!'

She had no sooner finished speaking than she wondered, did Mr. Fred admire Miss Lawrance? She felt an odd sort of pang.

'Do you think her pretty, mother?' she asked, in a faltering voice.

'Ay, ay; she's a real lady and no mistake; as pale as wax; and a train to her dress, did you see? I suppose it's French fashions.'

Mrs. Williams, who had no great tenacity of ideas, went out on a new line

of fancies ; her daughter pondered vaguely
on the differences between herself and Miss
Lawrance.   Mr. Fred could not have liked
her looks, or he would not have let his
mother insult the poor thing.   That was
not nice of him ; she blamed him gravely.
What a venturesome pleasure it is, fraught
with how delicious a sense of self-assertion
and independence, to dare to blame those
on whom we secretly know that all our
peace of mind depends !

They reached the little iron gate that
opened on their neat flower-garden.   Mrs.
Williams stopped to bind up some draggling
sprays of rose, for on Sundays she liked
being in the garden, there was so much
coming and going along the highway.
Susie did not wait ; she ran through the
dark parlour, always dim with its black
oak lining ; on the table at one end the
ledgers and account books were neatly set
out, she sighed as she looked at them and
shook her head ; but she did not stop ; she

hurried upstairs into her bedroom, and sat
down at the foot of the bed. Nothing
had happened, yet her blood was whirring
through her veins, her head felt dizzy and
full. She dropped it into her hands and
sat gazing at the floor. She felt strangely
reluctant to go this evening; yet her heart
was throbbing with wild joy and expectation. She had not done it, she kept saying
to herself, her mother had done it—but her
mother did not know what this meeting
must mean to Mr. Fred, what it meant to
her. A whole language of looks and tones,
a whole beseeching and granting unper-
ceived by her mother, had passed between
them in those few minutes. Susie felt that
her mother had unconsciously betrayed
her, against her will, but according to her
desire. She had been handed over, so to
speak, to a mastering fate. Now there
was nothing to do but fear, hope, expect.
Ah, she should see him again this evening;
hear his voice, feel his sleeve against her

arm.   Did he love her, or did he only like her?   She did not doubt but she should know.

You, my reader, may question that a girl of strong good sense and sterling character should love, however favouring the circumstance, a mere handsome unprincipled scapegrace such as Fred Masters; but it is no less a fact that often the most reasonable and conscientious persons are at the same time hot in feeling, headstrong in passion, and capable of running all risks in love.

Sweet, impressionable Arden, so much less strong-minded, would have had too delicate a judgment to fall in love with such a man.   She possessed neither the force of self-abnegation nor the intensity of sentiment which might lead Susie Williams hopelessly astray, or at last condemn her to a heart-breaking renunciation.   Poor girl; she loved strongly, and suffered none the less in suspecting her love to be im-

prudently wasted. During these three
months, in which so little had been said,
so much hinted, she had striven by all
means in her power to break loose from
the strengthening chain; now she had been
bound against her will. She would struggle
no more. She would wait and see.

The door at the top of the staircase was
opened. 'Susie!' called her mother.

'Yes, mother.'

'Harry's stayed tea to Farmer Willis's.
It's almost six o' the clock; you'd better
come down and get your tea with me.'

'I'm coming.'

She took off her bonnet, threw it
hurriedly on the bed, and rushed downstairs.

'Why, Susie,' cried Mrs. Williams,
'what a fright you look, girl! Aren't
you going to smarten yourself up a bit
afore you go to church?'

'I shall do.'

'And your hair all anyhow, and your

face as long as if you were going to a
funeral. I don't call it respectful.'

'It's my voice they want, not my
face.'

'I dare say—but when the Squire's son
offers to see you home.'

'Advancement! treasure! The duke's
son!' quoth Susie bitterly, who was read
in Lamb's selections. Then as the whole
meaning of the passage flashed on her—
'Oh, mother, mother dear, I beg your
pardon.'

'Ay, you are too often rude to your
mother, Susie. Some day you'll be sorry.'

'I'm sorry now, mother.'

'Well, then, make yourself look pretty
to please me; you'll never be younger.'

'Not to-night, mother dear.' She got
up and kissed her mother; then taking
down a long blue waterproof and a straw
hat from a peg by the door, she put them
on.

'Susie!' cried Mrs. Williams, horrified;

' what's come to you? You're never going to church in your garden things! '

' Yes, mother.'

She shut the door softly, and was gone. Out in the lane where the light was dim, and the sky turning a soft yellow-green behind the tall Scotch firs—out in the quiet lane she felt a childish pang of regret that she had not pleased her mother, or rather that Mr. Fred would see her looking so ugly and shabby. Her blue eyes —widened with anxiety and expectation— looked out forlornly from under the brown straw brim, the blue cloak hung gracefully enough round the slender little figure; but, when she passed the canal by the field-path to church, she could not refrain from bending over, to glance at her own reflection. How common and plain she thought herself. She was almost ready to turn back with vexation. But this mood, so foreign to her character, veered round suddenly, and gave way to an outbreak of her natural pride. It was on purpose she had refrained from looking her best—she would scorn to attract, to entangle him. He should know and see the difference between them, the gulf that divided her, in all matters of outward show, from his sisters or Miss Lawrance. It was no priggish book-learned phrase, it was one of the strongest instincts of her nature that had prompted Susie when she had said: 'One must love institutions.' Nothing was clearer, more universal a duty, to her thinking, than that every class should progress, should perfect itself in its own groove, remaining distinct and respectable. Not that she formulated her theory, but it was no less a motive of her actions. It was this that made her work so hard to reinstate her family in their inherited condition of comfort and consideration. It was this that made her feel her love for Fred Masters to be unlawful and unfortunate. It was an upheaval of her convictions.

Meanwhile it was in quite a different mood that Fred thought of the approaching meeting. From his point of view there was no harm in it. He certainly did not intend to marry Susie Williams, but neither had he any more sinister designs upon her. She was the prettiest girl in the village, and he the young Squire. It was natural that each should contribute to the amusement of the other.

Besides, he really liked Susie Williams. Her vehement downrightness and simplicity attracted him by the very force of contrasts, and had she been in his own rank of life he would certainly have married her. That was unfortunately impossible; but he could see no reason why a fellow should not make love to a farmer's pretty sister. And, depend upon it, a girl like Susie Williams would know how to take care of herself. That was her lookout.

So he finished his cigar. Sunday was

certainly a dull day at the Hall. The
hours lagged and dragged as if it would
always be afternoon. Fred became quite
excited as the evening drew on at last.
He sat smoking after tea and thinking
what he would say to Susie. She was a
sweet little soul, so frank and honest ; nor
did it once occur to him that he was doing
his best to spoil her frankness. She was
certainly the prettiest girl he knew, so
slim and fair and rosy. And such a child,
a man might express a liking for her
without committing himself. Susie should
never be the worse for his affection. So
Fred mused, feeling very virtuous and at
peace with all the world, as he lounged
in the great garden chair under the acacia
tree. He was so comfortable that he let
the time pass on till, on pulling out his
watch, he discovered that service must be
nearly over. Then he strolled leisurely
towards the church.

The door was open for the sake of the

air ; the clear voices of the choir sounded far down the lane. Fred walked across the churchyard and looked in. Yes; Susie was there. Not, however, as he had expected and wished to see her, casting anxious glances towards the door, wondering why he did not come. They were practising a difficult anthem. The schoolmaster had not come, and Susie was alto, conductor, and organist at once. She stood by the organ, turning round every now and then to play with her full firm touch some single phrase or motive, and then the labour began of getting it sung in time. She had forgotten everything but the task in hand ; her brows were knit, there was resolution in her face and bearing. She had pushed back her hat, her pretty yellow hair rippled over her temples ; her cloak was thrown back over her shoulders that she might beat time more freely. ' Listen,' she said, and sang the difficult phrase herself in all the parts, one after another.

Then an awful Babel began, as the choir essayed to put it together, Susie becoming more in earnest, more dominant, more successful, till at last the phrase was repeated correct in time and harmony.

'That's well,' cried Susie; 'now sing it all through.' Then she turned to the instrument and began to play, and the anthem went smoothly enough; her voice, her playing, directing all. Fred, standing in the shadow of the doorway, watched her, not without a certain impatience; never had she seemed so difficult to obtain, so necessary, so distant, before. Here she seemed so perfectly mistress of herself, so able to direct, command. Would she indeed submit to his passion? She should, she should! A sort of fury of desire awoke in him as he looked on while she directed this confusion, calmly, skilfully, quite unconscious of his presence. At last it was all over; he shrank into the shade; the choir passed out slowly, one by one; then, last of all, alone, a little sadly, she also came. He put out his hand. ' Susie ! ' he whispered.

She did not hear, but he could see that her face was changed to a tearful, childlike sorrow ; that she huddled her arms in her cloak as if it were mid-winter.

' Susie ! ' he said.

' Ah, you are come ! '

She gave him her hand ; he drew it closer towards him, drew her to his breast, folded her in his arms, looking at the sweet upturned face. She was really very pretty.

It was the first time he had called her by her name, the first time he had ignored the ordinary friendly greeting ; he had never yet told her that he loved her, and yet she did not feel surprised. She continued to look up at him with timid questioning eyes.

Then he stooped and kissed her.

'I am so glad you kissed me first in church,' she said.

The simple speech seemed to sting him; he loosed his hold of her for a moment. Then he caught her to him passionately, defiantly, kissing her hair, her eyes, her mouth. 'I love you, Susie,' he cried; 'I love you, I love you——'

'Think,' she cried; it was as if she were sinking to sleep in the snow and made one supreme struggle for life, 'think of all there is between us. Your place, my place—how far apart.' She held up her arms and kept him from her while she spoke, so that he might let her finish, might hear her through.

'Does that prevent me loving you?' he cried. She felt his arms round her again; there was no more struggling now.

'I love you,' she whispered.

Ah, she was wild with joy; she could have cried it out to the stars, to the trees, to the wind, only that he was by her side to hear. There was but one cloud on her delight: he had forbidden her just yet to say a word to mother or brother about their secret.

CHAPTER XI.

PICTURES.

For some days after that eventful Sunday Arden was quite worn out. All the fatigue, the recoil of memory, the perception of her own loneliness, seemed to weigh upon her together. It was very hot weather, for those few days almost as hot as Italy ; and Arden, like all people who have lived long in Italy, dreaded the heat, not knowing how soon it would be over and wished for again. So she sat on the verandah, talking to her grandfather, while Mrs. Lawrance, with tightening lips and greatening eyes, worked and listened in silence. Arden had offered to help in the work, though, to say the truth, she was not great in such matters ;

but Mrs. Lawrance had answered, somewhat grimly, that if Sylvia would only
do her own sewing that would be quite
enough ; that she had got used to working
alone.   She sighed a little.   Arden misunderstood her, and begged again and again
to be allowed to do something ; the elder
woman quietly refused ; her sigh had been
one of regret for those days gone by when
she was alone with her husband.   So,
glad of her enforced idleness, Arden leaned
back in her arm-chair, and talked, now and
then, of her old life, of her father and his
ways; showing, artlessly enough, how
much more to her mind they were than
the conduct of life at the Bushes.   Sometimes she would read ; but there were not
many books at the Bushes, save the
Classics, some works on engineering, and a
long file of the 'Gentleman's Magazine.'
It was not very entertaining.   And no
visitors ever came.   Still Arden hoped for
better things; she did not despond.   If

she could not continue her old interests, she made up her mind to seek for new ones.

We know that she had made up her mind to become a sort of stay of life to her grandparents, and when Mrs. Lawrance so curtly negatived her proposal to help in the indoor work, she quietly determined to look after the farming.

She knew very little about such matters, but after diligent perusal of a farm manual, she set out, one cooler morning, and walked over the little estate of thirty or forty acres. It was all grazing land and in bad condition; the high lands bare with great fissures, the lower part undrained, covered with coarse rank herbage. The farm man roused himself from sleep to tell her that 'the grass was so mortal scarce this year, he had put the cows in the smallest hay-meadow.' There they were, browsing away with good-will, eating their winter's store. No wonder,

thought Arden, fresh from her farm manual
and fired with the zeal of a reformer, no
wonder Mrs. Lawrance complains they
bring her butter back from the market !

She went home, hot and tired indeed,
but foreseeing for herself a career of busy
usefulness.

'Grandpapa,' she said that afternoon, as
they sat in the verandah, 'do you know
the hill meadow is all full of cracks—I
could put my hand and arm in—and as dry
as a bone.'

'Well, well, Sylvie, we musn't complain, while there's enough for us to eat,
and there's so many in want.'

'It's allus so in summer ; 'tis the lack
o' rain.'

'And there's too much rain in the front
meadow,' cried Arden. 'A sort of marsh,
all thick-stemmed lily roots.'

'Ah well, the cows must take it turn
and turn about; the one in hot weather,
Sylvie, the other in dry ! '

'But, grandpapa,' she pursued, 'the cows are in neither now; they're in the hay-meadow.'

'Dear, dear!' said Mrs. Lawrence; 'and last winter we spent twenty pound in hay; the pasture's got that thin and poor, there's no nourishment in it!'

'It 'll last our time,' sighed the old man; 'it 'll last our time, Nannie.'

'The manual says,' went on Arden in a shy impersonal tone, 'that if the hill meadow were to be dug up and turned over, let lie fallow for a year and then sown, it would make a beautiful pasture. After all, grass is a sort of crop, isn't it, grandpa?'

'I'm not one for changing and shifting,' he said; 'let well alone, Sylvie; there are two proverbs would guide you through most of the circumstances of life. One is "Let well alone," and the other "Let sleeping dogs lie."'

'Thank Heaven,' cried Arden, 'every-

one does not think so, or the world would
be a sort of Hospital for Incurables!'

'Softly, softly, my dear,' said the old
man.

But Mrs. Lawrance would not overlook
Arden's impetuous speech.

'I wonder at you, Sylvie! Lecturing
your gran'pa as if he was a three-years
child; you as has no esperience of ageri-
culter; and then you infarm us we're
incurables! I suppose it's a very different
sart a' life from what you're accustomed to
in furrin parts; but if it wasn't for your
gran'pa, what would 'a become of you, for
all your fine acquaintance? I never could
abide ingratitood and sarce!' The last
phrase, it is only fair to admit, was intended
to be *sotto voce*, although clearly audible.
Arden had too much sense to be angry.
She perceived there was a great deal of
truth in Mrs. Lawrance's criticism, and
leaned towards her, speaking eagerly :

'Oh, please don't think so! Indeed I

am not ungrateful. It's just because I feel you are so good to me, you and grandpapa, and offered me a home when no one else did, though you knew nothing about me; that's just why I want to be of some use to you, and not only in the way and an encumbrance.'

'I'm sure, Sylvie, if you allus spoke as pretty, there'd be nothing to complain of,' replied the elder woman, almost affectionately.

'Perhaps I shall improve,' said Arden, wistfully.

'To be sure she will,' cried her grandfather, delighted at this sudden dispersion of a threatened fuss; 'to be sure she will; in six months she'll be a sensible redcheeked English country girl. Why, she looks better already, I believe, and Rome wasn't built in a day, was it Sylvie?'

'Ah, don't let us talk of Rome.'

Indeed, even to think of Rome was dangerous; such a mist of tears would flood her eyes, her heart would sink so, and a ball grow in her throat till she almost choked. But she would not have lost one pang of those bitter-sweet poignant memories; as even pain is welcome in a numbed limb, as any sight is longed for by blinded eyes, and one gone deaf would be thankful, indeed, to hear the screeching of a night-jar, so in this cold senseless present Arden greeted those aching memories which were the only part of her life that seemed alive still and capable of sensation.

One day, when she felt stronger, and when, as usual, there was nothing for her to do except to keep out of the way, she went upstairs into the attic-loft, and opened one of her great trunks, hitherto untouched. There lay her easel, her palette, and painting tools; there were her sketches made under her father's supervision, and some notes of his also, studies for his larger painting; she took them tenderly in her arms and carried them into her room.

There was one of Ponte Molle, green and desolate. There was a corner of some hill-town, weather-stained white houses, with little towers, projecting roofs, uneven loggie and terraces, a tall cypress, a wide view below. Then came studies of roads and oliveyards. Then one which made her heart beat faster and the tears fall like rain ; the purple-flowered Piazza at Torcello, with the grey old buildings round. The brushmarks were still fresh, the paint scarcely dried in. How different the world was when that sketch was painted !

It was just before she had met the Roses in San Marco. She had not been thinking very much of her father then ; she had been so glad to meet them. And yet now, no one seemed worth caring for much, because he was dead ; she recalled, crying softly, the day they had gone to Torcello ; the last happy morning of his

life. Then her father's death ; and she
had been very desolate and lonely, and conscious that she belonged to no one. Then
she had been told that her grandfather had
asked her to come and live with him.
After all he must have cared for her more
than those others cared who had known
her all her life, who had petted and spoiled
her. He was very kind. But perhaps he
had only invited her from a sense of duty.
Why, then, he must be very good.

With a rush of tender feeling towards
him, she took up her father's sketches and
hurried downstairs.

Her grandfather was asleep in his great
arm-chair in the little library, where he
read his paper and pretended now and then
to look over the accounts of income and
expenditure. Arden did not go away ; she
crept softly to the window and sat down,
still holding the sketches on her lap.
She looked at her grandfather's sleeping
face. How good and honourable it looked

in its repose, though the forehead and chin
told of obstinacy and prejudice, though the
slackened limbs betrayed a habit of indolent days.   But age, bringing out these
characteristics, had also revealed a nature
upright and truthful ; ever ready to help,
though not eager to help; habitually
generous in thought, prevented only by
unvanquished circumstance and a natural
supineness from being as generous in deed.
Arden thought it a face to love ; it re-
minded her, notwithstanding much unlike-
ness, of her own father. The tears gathered
into her eyes.   She turned away and
looked out.   There was a little breeze
outside ; the great lilac bushes before the
window softly rustled their heart-shaped
leaves.   On the other side the drive, the
little lawn was hedged in with apple-trees ;
under their shade the yellow beehives were
ranged, and the bees were flitting to and
fro over the flower-borders among the tall
hollyhocks and lingering white lilies, the

phlox and stocks and carnations, the roses
and poppies. She could hear their busy
hum where she sat.   A fish leapt in the
pond under the apple and quince branches,
making a clear cool plop in the water.
Some errant hens and chickens were peck-
ing at the gravel.   Everything wore a look
of indescribable peace.

'After all, I shall be happy here,' said
Arden.

Thoughtlessly she spoke aloud, and her
voice roused the old man from his doze.
He opened his eyes and looked round.

'Sylvie!'

'Yes, grandpapa.'   She got up and
went to his side, taking the pochades with
her.   'I've brought you some of papa's
sketches to see.'

'John's work?' Mr. Lawrance sat up;
'of course, of course.   Where are my
glasses, Sylvie?'

'Here, grandpapa; see, this is near
Rome—isn't it beautiful?'

He did not seem so satisfied, turning from one sketch to another, looking at them from all points of view.

'But don't you like them, grandpapa?' she asked.

'Well, well, Sylvie; I'm no judge; people painted differently in my time; they look too bleak and grey and white for me. Give me old Crome and Constable for landscape.'

'Ah, I never saw them,' said Arden. 'No doubt they are great painters, too.'

'You may well say so. Ah, I used to be reckoned quite a judge of painting; but mind I'm not disparaging John's work; he had the knowledge no doubt, poor fellow—he had the knowledge. But it takes us old folk some time to get used to new styles.'

'Still, papa was a great painter.'

'No doubt, poor fellow, no doubt.'

Arden felt a little dissatisfied all the same. The pictures *were* good, she felt sure.

She stood looking at them herself, with a sort of vague idea that her father's work must not be set aside disregarded, that if her grandfather did not admire it she must redouble her admiration.

She was still looking at them, while her grandfather dozed off again, when the door opened, and Mrs. Lawrance came in.

'Hush!' said Arden, 'grandpa's asleep.'

She came to the door with her treasures in her arms.

'Can I do anything?' she said.

'No; ail's done now, Sylvie. What have you got there?'

'Pictures—papa did them.'

'Let's see! Why they're not picters, Sylvie, they're views.'

'Yes; Italy.'

'Good law, what a desolate place!'

'Mrs. Lawrance!'

'Just think of it. I allus heerd say Italy was a land of Canaan, flowing with ile and wine.'

' So it is.'

' Why, Sylvie, how can you say so and look at it—aäl commons and cypresses and whited sepulchres ; it seems like a sort of cemetery.'

' It's that too,' said Arden.

' I'm sure I can't see why you should pine after it so, then ; there's more beauty in the view from Mrs. Masters' gate—and they come aäl the way from Birmingham to make draughts of it. Why don't you paint it, Sylvie, come now?'

' True. I might as well be doing some-thing.'

' It 'ud be a nice enjyment for you ; there's lots to paint in Arden prettier than those.'

Although Arden was not converted to this desirable opinion, yet she welcomed the idea of setting to paint. She had no great talent ; but she had been well-taught, and had a fine natural sense of colour and the relations of tone. Once, at some pro-

vincial Italian exhibition she had sold a
sketch for 100 lire ; certainly that was
not much, though she had been very proud
of earning it. But now it would be a
matter of real relief and importance to her,
to earn at least enough for her pocket-
money. To be dependent is always bitter,
save to depend on those we love ; but to be
dependent and idle is shameful. At least,
Arden thought so.

She coloured up to the roots of her
hair.

' I could try,' she said. ' I would like
to paint something simple—a river, some
thin trees.'

' There's no water hereabouts, Sylvie,
save the canal. But it's as pretty as heart
can wish on Sunday mornings, with the
bells aäl a-ringing, and the barges going up
and down, and the mint and wild flowers
smelling as sweet as a garden.'

' You see, I couldn't paint all that.'

' Maybe not ; but why should you

paint thin trees, when the finest trees in England are aäl round for miles?'

'They're so difficult.'

'That may be—but who'd buy portraits of scanty trees, Sylvie? Better take a considerable deal of trouble and produce summut worth the pains.'

'True.'

Mrs. Lawrance was glad that she had roused Arden to exert herself. Not that she had much opinion of painting, save as an 'enjyment,' and, to do her justice, she did not at all take into consideration the idea that Arden might sell her pictures, and help in that way to pay for her keep. But although, owing to some strange mixture of hospitality and hostility, she refused to allow the girl to be of any use, still it annoyed her beyond expression to watch the listless conduct of Arden's days, to see her reading without interest, or sitting, her pale hands crossed on her black skirt, silently thinking, or meddling with things that did not concern her ; or talking, day after day, to her grandfather, reviving in his heart the interests of a past in which his wife had no share. Besides, while she painted, the girl would be safely out of the house. Sufficient reasons (felt though not formulated) for welcoming the idea.

Arden, for her part, was quite as ready to relinquish her inaction. She looked so bright all dinner-time that her grandfather remarked her cheerful face.

'After dinner I am going to look out for a subject,' she announced.

'That's right, Sylvie ; landscape painting's the healthful work and healthful play at once.'

'It's so good of you to take an interest, grandpapa!'

'Is it? You see I'm thinking how gay you'll make our walls look.'

'Yes ; but I should like to expose one or two of the best sketches.'

'Expose them?'

'Send them to a gallery—an exhibition.'

'Oh, yes ; there's a first-rate local exhibition at Birmingham. It is a great place for artists, Birmingham.'

'Indeed, I never heard that. I am very glad.'

'Why yes, Sylvie. Baker was a Birmingham man.'

'Baker?'

'Yes, Baker—Baker the landscape painter.'

'Oh yes.' Then, after a pause, 'I feel so ashamed,' said Sylvie, 'when I think how little I know of your great painters. Of course papa always ranked as an Italian. Will you tell me about the English painters, grandpapa,—what sort of things they try to do, and so on?'

'All in good time, Sylvie, all in good time,' said Mr. Lawrance, rather nervously, remembering that his theories of art were chiefly derived from the notices in the *Birmingham Daily Post*.

'Ah, Sylvie!' cried Mrs. Lawrance, 'it isn't many a girl 'as such a grandpa. You can't be rightly said to know yet what a mint of infarmation 'e's possessed of. Many's the question I've put to him o' winter evenings, and never one, so to speak, unresponded. But there, he's allus reading and thinking, reading and thinking ; it's bad for 'is 'ealth I often tell 'im ; but 'e's ever been such a perusing man.'

'I'm sure he's very clever,' said Arden, looking affectionately at the old man. She took it all on trust, though she had never seen him read anything save the *Birmingham Post*. But then, she had never been celebrated for penetration ; she generally measured people by their own accounts of themselves.

'Oh, Sylvie! Sylvie!' said her grandfather, 'what's to become of my reason now there are two women to flatter me ?'

Mrs. Lawrance's face clouded ever so little. She did not quite approve that Arden should be spoken of as equally influential with herself. Her voice took a somewhat colder intonation.

'The 'eat of the day is over now, Sylvie,' she said. 'It's none too warm for you to begin making chice of a view!'

'Very well, Mrs. Lawrance—*Dunque, Signore, la rinverisco.*' She made a quaint little curtsey to her grandfather and was gone.

'I wish she'd leave aäf tarking that gibberish?' cried Mrs. Lawrance petulantly.

'Patience, Nannie, patience. After all she's a bit o' sunshine in the old house.'

'Did you find it so dull without her?'

Mr. Lawrance decided on the better part of valour; he shut his eyes, nodded his head; no man is expected to answer questions in his sleep.

Meanwhile Arden set off on her expedition. It was an afternoon in which all views are beautiful, a broad and golden light. Still it was not a place to paint ; there was no subject and a multitude of detail. Arden looked in vain, unable to fix her mind. There was a lovely group of firs, but she could not carry her easel so far. The poplar-bordered road was winding and graceful, but she could find no point of view that would take in the stems of the trees in the hedge, and their tops. She would rather never paint again than paint at Mrs. Masters' gate. Still she went on down the lane, walking slowly, and continually looking about her.

There was one spot she would indeed have liked to paint. It was the orchard belonging to the black and white farm-house where Susie Williams lived. The trees were old and gnarled, with twisted spreading branches, and so large that, though the trunks were at some distance from each other, the boughs were locked

together, laced and interlaced in a sort of
net. This low net or roof was covered
now with ripening apples of all kinds,
great green baking apples, scarcely tinged,
pippins, small russet ones for keeping,
delicate Americans for show. The sun
caught, here and there, these spots of
brilliant colour, intense or delicate, shining
out of the heavier green of the foliage ; it
struck, too, on the mossed trunks ; and in
sun and shade alike the grass was green
with the startling brightness of aftermath ;
in the tufts of tall grass still left unsheared
round the trees the delicate valerian spread
its snowy tracery. Beyond all this, one
saw in the distance the next field, yellow
with ripened corn. It was a picture of
abundance, colour, autumn.

Still Arden went on, for to paint the
orchard one would have to be inside ; a
deep ditch and a high hedge separated it
from the road ; and sitting down to paint
one would only see the tree-tops. She

walked for nearly a mile. She really could find nothing else. Tired and almost cross she turned her steps homewards.

As she was passing the orchard again she turned round, shading her eyes, for another glimpse. In the low sun it looked much prettier than before ; a girl in a pink cotton sun-bonnet was reaching to the lower branches and gathering apples. She had on a brown linsey gown and a many-coloured cotton apron. Arden sighed. It was really a charming subject.

She must have stood looking for several moments, for Susie finished picking her apples, gathered them in her apron and turned. Then she saw Arden. She smiled, with her sudden natural smile.

'How beautiful your orchard is !' cried Arden, answering the smile.

'Good evening, Miss Lawrance. I'm so glad you like it, Miss Lawrance. Won't you step inside and look at it, Miss Lawrance, before the sun's down?'

Susie was very shy and eager. She had made quite a heroine of Miss Lawrance.

'Thank you, I am very much obliged. I have never seen such beautiful apple-trees. How must I get in?' said Arden.

'Oh, Miss Lawrance, I beg your pardon, keeping you waiting in the road. This way—see, through the flower-garden in front of the house.'

Arden followed, admired the flowers. Susie chatted and laughed. Arden was quite flattered, the girl seemed so glad to see her. It was quite like old times, when the old ladies in Rome used to treat her like a princess in a story-book.

The two girls lingered talking in the apple-yard. Susie forgot her shyness; Arden felt quite gay.

'I was longing to come inside,' she said, 'as I was going down the road, but I did not like to ask.'

'If you knew how often I have wished to see you here!' Susie added—the words

had slipped out unawares—'I beg your
pardon, Miss Lawrance,' she added, 'I
didn't mean to take a liberty.'

'You are very good.' Arden took the
girl's hand and the tears came into her
eyes.

'Oh, Miss Lawrance,' Susie went on, 'I
would so like you, if you would, just when
you pass to look over the hedge sometimes
and see if I'm there, and say "good-day."'

'Would you? Will you let me come
and paint the orchard?'

'Paint the orchard! Will you, will
you? And may I come and look on?'

'I shall be so pleased——'

'And you will tell me about Rome?'

'By-and-by.'

'And you will really let me know you?'

'Certainly, my dear.'

'I have wished so much to know a real
lady! I beg your pardon, Miss Lawrance,
that sounds very horrid; but I mean—I
mean I know no one, no woman of my

own age. You see, the other farmers'
daughters are very different. I am not a
lady; but I care for different things—
books, Carlyle, music—oh dear, I can't
say it.'

'You have said it very well. I shall
be quite as glad, dear Miss Williams, to
talk with you as you to talk with me, for
I, too, know no one here, and things are
all very different.'

She sighed.

'I am so sorry,' said Susie, ardently|;
'if only I could prevent things!' She
was thinking of Mrs. Masters; but Arden
had forgotten Mrs. Masters.

'Good-bye,' she said, holding out her
hand; 'and may I come to-morrow?'

'May you! Will you?'

'Yes; and you shall come and look
on.'

'I will read. I will not interrupt you.'

'Very well. *A rivederci.*'

Arden went off, glad to have secured

the orchard, thinking also that Susie Williams was a very nice little girl. But Susie felt much more strongly.

Since her engagement to Fred Masters, for so she considered it, Susie had greatly felt the need of a friend. Not of a confidante, for that was forbidden her, but of someone of her own age and sex, subject to the same experiences and temptations. By the standard of such a person she might secretly measure her own conduct ; it was now too foreign to her own traditions, she was too conscious that her own judgment disapproved of it, for her not to desire a different tribunal. This was one reason, but there were others why Susie should welcome Arden's companionship. For one thing, as she had said, Arden was a lady, of the same class as Mr. Fred's sisters ; to know such a person would be an immense boon to her, Susie thought. She used to be so proud, this girl; she used to contrast herself with the

Misses Masters, and thinking of her round
of duties, her pursuits, her aims and
theirs; she used to be conscious of a certain
superiority. Yet, because a trivial good-
for-nothing youth ventured to disapprove of
her now and then, she was ready to throw
overboard all her independence, her un-
conventionality, her habits of thought, and
learn meekly enough to what standard she
must conform. These reasons were, it will
be observed, somewhat utilitarian : Arden
was to serve as a catspaw to something
better. But Susie had instincts as well as
reasons. One of these was violently, passionately, to assert herself on the side of anything unjustly treated. Another—which she
shares with many independent, intellectual,
and rather roughly mannered people—was
an extreme devotion to whatever is frail,
graceful, delicate, attaching. Arden, pale, in
her deep mourning ; Arden with her foreign
bearing and memories ; Arden treated
coldly, slighted, a stranger ; Arden with

her beautiful face and curling hair, her sweet voice and tall lithe figure; such an *Erscheinung* called forth all Susie's tenderness and chivalry. She went in to tea flushed and excited. Harry was seated on the settle, smoking, his feet stretched out cased in stoutest boots.

'Why, Susie, wench; you're as rosy as your apples!'

'I've seen Miss Lawrance.'

'Eh? She's a pleasant-faced young woman.'

'She's lovely!'

'That's about it.'

A pause; but Susie was eager to detail her good fortune.

'And she's as sweet to talk to as to look at.'

'What! Did tha speak to her?'

'Yes; she came into the orchard, she is going to paint it.'

'Our orchard?'

'Yes; to-morrow.'

'How did you come to ask her, Susie? It was making free, I fear.'

'Ask her! She asked me. She is a real painter; and I may look on and talk to her; she said she would like to know me.'

'I'm glad.'

Then there was another silence. At last Susie broke it—

'The tea's nearly drawn, Harry; will you come? Here's mother.'

'Eh?'

'Tea's ready. Are you deaf?'

Harry roused himself. His eyes fell on his boots.

'What a loon I am! I can't sit down with you and mother so rough and dirty. Don't wait, Susie; I won't be a moment.'

He was off.

'Heavens! fancy Harry turning tidy!' cried Susie. 'I can't think what's come over the lad.'

'At all events there's room for improve-

ment,' said Mrs. Williams, 'and I'm glad
he's about to begin. Come, Susie.'

The smart little elderly beauty stroked
and arranged her cap ribbons and seated
herself at the tea-table. Harry came in.
The talk, of course, was chiefly of Arden's
visit. Mrs. Williams was delighted that
Susie should have a chance of acquiring
that elegance in which she had not followed
her mother's example. She insisted that
to-morrow afternoon Susie must ask Miss
Lawrance in to tea.

'I'll go and look out the chaney tea-set,
this evening,' she asserted.

'Nay, mother,' said Harry. 'Let's not
force Miss Lawrance to know us. All in
good time. She only asked to paint the
orchard.'

'I'm sure I don't see, Harry, as you
should stand in Susie's light—and she in
such luck with her friends.'

'In such luck?'

'Ay, with Mr. Fred, and now Miss

Lawrance. That comes of having a mother who's lived among the gentry—or your conceited old mammie thinks so, my Susie!'

'But what has Mr. Fred to do with it?' asked Harry. 'I don't like Mr. Fred; that's quite another matter.'

'Don't be so stiffnecked, Harry,' said Mrs. Williams.

Susie was as red as a turkey-cock.

'He helps me with my class at Sunday school,' she said; 'at least once or twice he did.'

'Ah!'—Harry relapsed into a dreamy silence. Conversation flagged. Even the pert and lively Mrs. Williams only tossed her head now and then, and suggested making tea-cakes. Susie said nothing; hot, and red, and indignant with herself and Fred. She knew she had told a lie. Unless she had broken a promise she could not have told the truth.

CHAPTER XII.

A LETTER AND A MEETING.

But Arden did not keep her promise. She had over-tired herself with her long walk in the heat, and for several days lay restless and fevered, on the sofa in the dark little dining-room, while Mrs. Lawrance waited on her with more anxiety and tenderness than the motherless girl had ever known.

'Ah, if you were always like this!' Arden cried one day. She knew she might be as petulant and familiar as she chose while she was ill.

'And if you was allus like this, Sylvie!' Mrs. Lawrance answered.

But Arden could not always be ailing

and dependent, nor even for long. Her nervous buoyant nature soon recovered from depression, and while she was still too ill to go out painting, she was well enough to assist herself, talk and laugh, and engross her grandfather's attention, and put an end to her temporary friendship with his wife.

Meanwhile she was missed at the Farm. Mrs. Williams was very plaintive over her wasted sally-lunns; Harry, too, though he did not complain, looked blank and disappointed. Susie made no excuse for her heroine, smiled, thought it quite natural, did not doubt but she would come to-morrow. Then to-morrow. Still to-morrow; when the others had forgotten their expectations.

It was really Susie who missed her most. The moment had come to her that comes to all, though very few perceive it; the moment when a passion that seems established for good or evil in our lives,

well known already to our hearts, comes
into collision with an unexpected force:
will, reason, conscience, call it as you may.
We had imagined all decision over. The
feeling is not so very new, nor yet so very
old ; we are in the full zenith of possession.
Then something cries to us : ' Is this
your choice? Mostly we do not hear, or
we answer, yes ; scarcely heeding, or ima-
gining that the decision has been already
made. But some hear ; some search and
keep, and their approved love is the dearer
to. them. And some reject with breaking
hearts, entering into the kingdom of God
free of disease, but maimed. Susie was
experiencing this renewal of choice. She
was anxious to escape from it into any
new interest. If Arden would only come,
either the inquiry might be dulled, or her
interest diverted, or at least she might
make some sort of shelter for herself,
something to break the dreariness and
bleakness, the coldness and utter desolation

of the altered world. But day after day lengthened, lagged, and passed by, and Arden did not come : Susie was left to decide the question for herself.

It was not so difficult to determine, that to deceive, however unwillingly, her mother and her brother, was cowardly and dishonourable. Susie always set out for the school—she would never consent to a more private tryst—with the intention of telling her lover that she could no longer endure this systematised dissimulation. But when she came in and saw Fred at the head of his class, or more often restlessly loafing about and shouting out occasional directions ; when she saw this bored, dull, heavy young fellow, suddenly look alive with content and animation at the first rustle of her dress, then Susie's heart failed, and her conscience threw up its brief and turned her lover's advocate. Indeed she did not know what would become of him without her. Oddly enough this consciousness that Fred was feeble, unprincipled, easily swayed, did not shock this strongly-fibred and resolute girl ; the knowledge that he needed her was the essential thing; without that she would never have consented to sacrifice her duty and her honour to his desire.

So on Sunday she began—

'Are you ill, Fred? you looked so tired, I thought, this morning.'

'Before you came?'

'I did'nt see you then; no, afterwards."

'No; I'm only bored.'

'Oh! why are you bored?'

'It's precious dull life for a fellow; loafing about from Sunday night till Sunday morning with nothing to look forward to. I tell you I can't stand it, Susie : do you hear?'

'I'm sure I wish you wouldn't stand it, dear Fred.'

'Ah, my dear little girl!'

'Wait before you kiss me ; let me explain—I mean, let me tell Harry.'

'Tell Harry!   There you are again with your conditions. You love your pride much more than you love me ! '

'Oh, Fred, there's nothing, nothing else I wouldn't do.'

'That's what women always say ; nothing but the one thing required of them.'

'Oh, Fred.   Don't you think I want to see you as much as you want to see me ? '

'Then why on earth do you make such a fuss ! '

'Because——'

'Because you'd rather break my heart than submit.'

The sense of injustice spurred Susie on to finish her sentence.

'Because it would be mean beyond words ! '

'You think I'm mean then ; eh ? '

But Fred was so much tickled with the

supreme ludicrousness of this idea, that he required no answer to his question. His laugh put him in good humour. · It must be owned that, in such a mood, Fred Masters had the sort of irresponsible, appealing, petulant and caressing charm which very selfish people sometimes possess; each one of his bright looks and words was a subtle flattery to Susie, and told her that he was so well-contented because she was at his side. She felt so necessary to him ; she alone made him look so happy, and he was so seldom happy ; how could she shatter this momentary delight of his by what she secretly felt would be a vain appeal to his sense of justice and responsibility? Indeed, he seemed a being of a different sphere, for whom those stern names need have no meaning.

So Susie deferred renewing the discussion till the hour of parting came.

'Now, Susie, Susie dear, do be kind. Let me see you for a little half-hour on Tuesday in the rickyard.'

'It can't be!'

'Oh, my love, how can you leave me to drag through all the live-long week without you! I can't keep straight without you, that's the truth.'

'Fred! Fred!'

'Well, it's your fault. I never pretended to be good ; but I might be good if you would help me—and you won't help me.'

'Not to dishonour, Fred.'

'Well, Susie ; the responsibility's yours. I shall be there, wet or fine.'

'I shall be indoors ; come and see me.'

'Bother ; and if you don't come to meet me, I shall be wild with despair.'

'Then don't come.'

'And very likely I shall get drunk again, and there'll be another row with the governor.'

'Now, Fred, you make me angry— good-bye!' cried the young girl.

'Oh, Susie, Susie, Susie! don't be so harsh. There, forgive me, dearest, I'll think of you and not give way. Only you shouldn't leave me so long alone—not till next Sunday, Susie?'

'Not till next Sunday.'

'Then good-bye; I shall be there on Tuesday, if you relent.'

'And I shall be at home, if you choose to come and find me.'

'One kiss, darling; good-bye!'

'Good-bye!'

And Susie walking off felt that she had gained a difficult victory in not sinking lower. So impossible did she find it to recover the original lost footstep.

But this consciousness of having fallen lower than her natural standing-point was a very sad and irritating one to her. Day by day she got less satisfied, less cheerful and hopeful than of old; alternately snappish and overwhelmingly contrite. The full round of daily duties in which she had formerly found a healthy pleasure, became a wearying, insupportable tax, now that

all her energies were bent on revolving a
question, much more absorbing and quite
foreign to the churning, and baking, and
brewing, and strict keeping of accounts.
It must be owned that these occupations
suffered by Susie's distraction ; but Susie
suffered too. She knew what it was to
wake in a morning and wish she had been
a chair, a table—any of the insensate fur-
niture on which she looked, that would not
have to think and feel, to decide and labour.
After a restless night, she began the day
weary and disheartened ; her little suc-
cesses seemed no longer real ; her little
failures seemed crushing despairs. It was
an effort to drag about. She counted every
step ; if Harry did not come in to dinner,
and she had to go and fetch him—it was
no longer a buoyant, eager companion who
ran out to meet him; sometimes he scarcely
recognised the lagging gait, the downcast
head. And now no longer in the evenings
she took out her book and toiled merrily at

the Siege of Dinant or followed the fortunes of Frederick of Prussia; propped in one corner of the settle, her eyes closed, her hands before her, she would sit in listless idleness, neither attempting to join in the family discussions, nor heeding the anxious looks that her mother and Harry would cast at her from time to time.

One such evening Mrs. Williams, after much uneasiness, suddenly smiled. It was evident she had a bright thought.

'Harry,' she said, 'I should take it very kind if you'd just step in the front garden and look at that new bed.'

'Now, mother?'

'Yes, yes, Harry, now,' cried little Mrs. Williams, nodding and shaking her cap ribbons at Susie, inert and weary, on the settle.

'Here I am.' He got up, gave himself a shake as if to shake off all remnants of his comfortable drowsiness, and followed her out of doors.

His step-mother led him towards the gate. It was very clear and still; the tree-tops scarcely swayed; the sky was full of light, and flecked with fleecy wathes of cloud.

Harry looked up. 'There'll be wind to-night,' he said.

'Oh, Harry, Harry. You think o' nothing but crops and weather.'

'But the rick's not thatched yet,' said her step-son, stupidly excusing himself.

'And if we lose a dozen ricks, where's the ruin compared to losing Susie?'

'Losing Susie!'

'Yes, you stupid goose, losing Susie! There, you look as if I thought the wind 'ud carry her away with the ricks, and I'm sure it might, she's got so thin o' late. But that's not what I meant.'

'Oh, mother, don't trifle with me; what is it?'

'Ay, you may well say so, that's the question. Whatever it be, she's as changed

as changed, our bright Susie; to see how
she sits and mopes ; and my heart comes
into my mouth every time I speak to her,
she snaps one up so.'

'She's sorely changed, poor child ;
poor little wench. D'ye think she's in
love?'

'Not seriously, or she'd have told me.
She always tells me everything, does Susie.'

' Is she ill, then ?'

' Ill, partly ; and in love, partly.   She's
slipped out of health somehow, and if we
don't take care, Harry, you and I, she'll
slip into an early grave.'

' Don't, mother.'

'But I must. I've been thinking ;
the worst of it is, we can do nothing, we
two ; she's too used to us.   And if I was
to say to her, " Susie, what is it, dear?"
either she'd answer nothing, or she'd become suspicious and think us spies upon
her.'

' It's dreadful,' said Harry, wiping his

forehead with his hand. 'Dreadful. I feel quite moithered-like.'

'Not I. 'Twill all come right in time. We'll see our Susie proud and happy yet. What's to do now is, write to that strange young lady at the Bushes and ask her in to tea.'

'Ask Miss Lawrance to tea?'

'Lord-a-mercy, Harry, will you never do anything but gape and wonder? Susie must have a change. Shall we hire a house at Leamington, or would you like me to ask Mrs. Masters to dinner?'

'Don't take one up so, mother; I think you're very clever. I should never have ventured.'

'Ventured! forsooth. And Susie moping and fretting herself to a shadow.'

'I'm sure I'm very grateful to you, mother.'

'Why, Harry, you're as red as a turkey-cock. Do you think it taking such liberty? Well, I'm sure; and to think of the gentlefolk I've known.'

' Shall we go in now? '

' Yes ; but mind, never a word to Susie until we're sure of Miss Lawrance.'

So they turned towards the darkness of the porch.

Mrs. Williams exerted consummate generalship to get Susie to go to bed soon after eight o'clock. Then she tripped about the room, quite brisk and excited, hunting up her seldom-used papier-maché writing-desk, the inkstand, the mother-o'-pearl penholder, · the blotting-book with ' A Present from Tunbridge ' on the back, the jar of shot to dry the pen in, the packet of vari-coloured sheets with scolloped edges, the much-referred-to dictionary ; all the ornamental appurtenances of a semi-genteel writing-table.

Finally these long-treasured objects were spread out on a page of the *Field* upon the table, so that no inkspots might disfigure the neat red cloth. Mrs. Williams hovered about, looking at them with clasped

hands, as though she might derive inspira-
tion from the very sight of them.   At last
she took a chair, set it very straight, laid
her cheek in her palm and composed herself to meditation.   Finally she took her
pen swiftly, as though to record some
brilliant thought, but it was only to write
‘ Woodleigh Farm, July 15th.’

‘ Pity it hasn’t a good name.   Williams’
Farm is more than I’ll consent to write,
but were it called th’ Oaks or th’ Ashes
t’ud be a thousand times more genteel.’

‘ But there’s no good oak nearer than
Feversham Spinny ; and, I thank my stars,
no ashes to spile my crops.’

‘ Lor’, Harry, how you worry.   Let be,
now—

‘ Woodleigh Farm, July 15th.

‘ DEAR MISS LAWRANCE——’

‘ Wouldn’t it be more civil-like to
begin, Honoured Miss ? ’

‘ Lor’, Harry, how low that ’ud be,
now !   Listen—

'Dear Miss Lawrance,—I seize the opportunity——'

'All the letters I ever wrote began, "I take up my pen" or "this comes hoping,"' demurred Harry.

'What a plough-boy style. No.—I seize the opportunity (ah, two p's) having heard from my daughter as you expressed a wish——'

'That's good!' said Harry; '"expressed a wish." Lor', mother, you've got it all at your fingers' ends.'

'Expressed a wish,' meditated Mrs. Williams. 'Now listen, Harry—having heard from my daughter as you expressed a wish to pourtray our humble orchard——'

'Lor', mother, it's like a penny-reading.'

'Our humble orchard,' went on Mrs. Williams, nodding and smiling with tears of pride in her china-blue eyes. 'To beg you to visit our little——'

'Home,' suggested Harry.

'Nonsense ; don't spoil it.   There, I've got it—

'Our little homestead, any day which it may suit your convenience to mention——'

'But there's nothing about Susie?'

'Of course there's nothing about Susie.—Requesting the favour of a reply —that's to ensure her coming, you see, Harry.'

'It's like a lawyer!' cried Harry.

'Madam, I obediently remain,

'Yours truly,

'SARIANNA WILLIAMS,

'*née* WELLAND.'

'*Née's* the French for maiden name,' added Mrs. Williams, whose French, the result of six months' residence at a convent school some twenty years ago, was little more than a dim memory.

All the same the French word, the pink and scented note, the fine phrases, all served to dazzle Harry, whose own inspi-

ration would scarcely have prompted more
than 'Honoured Miss, this comes hoping
you will come to tea to-morrow evening. Your obedient servant, Henry
Williams.' Having this abortive missive
in his mind, he felt the superiority of his
step-mother's production. That was, he
imagined, just the sort of communication
to address to Miss Lawrance ; coloured and
scented, foreign and fine. With what disdain would she not look on their plain,
comfortable parlour. For the first time
Harry blushed as he looked round him ;
somehow all the merit seemed to have
gone out of the inherited and sober home,
of which he had always been so proud.

'I 'most fear it's taking a liberty,
mother ; we're but unkéd folk, and she so
fine.'

'Nonsense ; unkéd indeed ! Speak
for yourself, sir. It's a thousand pities you
left off your schooling at fifteen.'

'T'wasn't my fault,' growled Harry ;

and indeed it was stinging to be twitted
for a lack of learning which was only the
result of a self-sacrifice to his father's
interests.

Mrs. Williams felt contrite.

'There, there,' she said, 'you're better
than most, any way.   Now, Harry, see
that Curtis leaves this letter at the Bushes
first thing to-morrow morning.'

'I'll see to it, mother.   Well, good-
night.'

'Good-night.'

Darkness and silence then invested the
parlour, and kept their watch over the
little rose-coloured letter, the fruit of such
patient labour, the seed of such anxious
hopes.

Meanwhile Susie tossed restlessly upstairs, unconscious of all that was being
done on her behalf, dreaming that all her
troubles were a dream, and that her life
was fair and straight and open as it used
to be.   And half a mile away Arden slept

a deep untroubled slumber, forgetting all the frets that had no secret blame or shame in them. With her black clothes lying empty near her, Arden, a stranger and fatherless, would have seemed most pitiable, could some all-penetrating Eye (as we see in old-fashioned Scripture pictures) have pierced to either chamber. And Arden thought so herself, and all the people in the village save one, who knew how much the worst of sorrow is an unguessed shame.

Arden woke the next morning, restless and eager. She was always gay and active in the morning, for until the postman brought the paper, or the small shopping, or a circular or stray note at eleven o'clock, Arden regularly expected a letter from the Roses. One short note, greeting her at her hotel in London, was all her news of them since she had left them at Venice. No wonder she thought it strange and was anxious, for in six weeks they seemed to have forgotten her ; these friends for whom she had forgotten her father, whom she had cared for all her life.

In the midst of her expectations and grumbles, her letter-writing to and letter-waiting from these earliest acquaintances, the people at the farm were but slightly remembered. Sometimes, indeed, she thought of Susie's bright face, and of the green and writhen orchard hung with coloured apples ; but as yet she felt little energy, and moreover, the longer she deferred, the redder the fruit would become.

So when she woke that morning it was only of Gerard and Ellie that she was thinking, beings as different in her eyes from Harry and Susie Williams as Ferdinand and Miranda from Falstaff and Anne Page. She came down to breakfast looking gay, but thoughtful.

'Good marning, Sylvie. Your gran'-papa's none so well this marning.'

'Oh, I'm sorry, Mrs. Lawrance.'

'I'd rather see you pleasant than sorry, child.'

'Yes, Mrs. Lawrance?'

Arden subsided into silent preoccupation.

'And what is it you're so thaätful over, Sylvie?'

'Here to London, one day; London to Paris, one night; Paris to Turin, twenty-four hours; Turin to Venice, one day—sixty hours.'

'What are you arter, Sylvie?'

'I might get an answer to my letter to-day.'

'Oh, Sylvie, Sylvie!'

'But there isn't anything wrong, Mrs. Lawrance, in wishing to hear from one's friends.'

'No; but when instead of being happy in the station of life the Lard's called us to, we're allus a'fretting and frabbing for summat else, and taking no notice, or neglecting aäl that's going on

about us—that's more discontent than
aught else, Sylvie.'

The tears came into Arden's eyes.

' Perhaps I am discontented,' she said,
very gently, ' but my life used to be very
different.'

She pushed her plate away, the bread
tasted bitter; her eyes, filled with tears,
did not see the brown-patterned wall and
the ivy-darkened window, but her old
home in Italy; her father's pleasant studio;
people coming in and out, the Roses among
them; herself, too, as she remembered herself in her father's picture, a gay, slim
creature, dressed in white, very young and
free of sorrow.

Mrs. Lawrance said nothing; she went
on with her breakfast, for much hard
work must be done between then and
dinner; but as she munched her food, and
gulped down her tea, she too was thinking
that her life used to be very different;
peaceful, quiet, orderly, economical. And

now there was Sylvie, always crying or laughing, or falling ill, never any use to anyone, nor any pleasure, either; taking the food and shelter given her with forced thanks and an unhappy face. Would to God her husband had let well alone and left the girl to be looked after by her own friends !

So while Arden was growing tender-hearted and miserable over her memories, Mrs. Lawrance, in her turn, was hardening herself to resent ingratitude. She finished her meal, got up and pushed her chair in its place against the wall.

Arden started, and got up.

' Can I be of any use, this morning?' she asked, mechanically.

' None, thank you,' said her step-mother, grimly ; and went away to look after the housework, the cooking, the beasts, and the dairy.

Arden sighed ; there was nothing to do or to look forward to, all day long, save the postman's visit.   She caught up her broad Tuscan hat, and set out to meet him.

'I wonder if they'll come to England this autumn,' she was saying to herself; 'and if they will come and see me, or if I may go and see them.   It's the sixteenth of July to-day.   They said they would be coming towards the end of August; just a month.   Oh, dear, how will it go?'

Then she walked on a little, spying to right and left, but there was no one in the lane; so she went towards the canal bridge—she would surely meet the postman soon.   As she walked, she went on with her reverie.

'If they were to ask me again, I would go with them.   I would get away from here and go to Italy.   One can live on little there, and I have forty pounds a-year.'

Pleased with this reverie, she stopped

on the roadside, leaning against a hurdle,
making pictures with her half-shut eyes.

'I would give lessons, and paint,' she
cried. 'Oh, if the Roses would come and
take me away from here!'

She sighed, but not with regret; rather
from the impatience of her eager hope.
And now, beyond the bridge, she could
hear the tramp of heavy boots. She
looked under the arch; the framed landscape of green-bordered road and lush
over-hanging elms was enlivened by a
figure—if the bent and dusty postman
could be called an enlivenment; to Arden
he certainly was—she ran to meet him.

'Any letters?' she cried, out of
breath.

'Good day, Miss: I'll foind th' News
for th' old gen'leman.'

'Nothing else?'

'Nothing else, Miss.'

He trudged on under the bridge, along
the level road. When he was fairly out

of sight, Arden sank down on a heap of stones and began to cry.

Arden had not been long on her throne of desolation, when she gradually became aware of a sort of shuffling sound on the road in front of her.   Her first impulse was to stop crying ; her next to pull her hat well over her eyes.   Then she looked up.

A farm-labourer, a slouching fellow, with hair and skin much the colour of his light-coloured and soiled fustian, was standing on the opposite side the road, looking at her with sheepish curiosity. Either to excite her attention, or from mere shyness, he kept on scuffling, first with one foot, then with the other, through a little heap of poplar down and fallen blossoms collected on the road- side.   As she looked at him, he suddenly brought this amusement to a close, and as suddenly jerked forward his right arm.   The great brown hand held a rose- coloured missive.

'What a clumsy Pierrot,' thought Arden, with an unexpected smile; thus encouraging the puppet into speech.

'Bean't yer th'old gen'leman's gran'-child?' he asked.

'Yes,' said Arden, smiling anew.

'Th' old Missus bade me hand yer this.' So speaking, he came a little forward, and threw, or rather shoved, the letter on to Arden's lap. She was still sitting on the heap of stones. While she was feeling for some coppers he shuffled off; but she saw him come up to her again. She thought it was for the money; but he did not come close, only near enough to speak without shouting.

'Doan't yer moind,' he said; 'and doan't yer get rheumatics on them stones.'

And before she could think of the money he was off.

His rude comfort had effectually dissipated Arden's gloom. She now began to wonder who 'th' old Missus' could be,

who sent such dainty missives by so
queer a messenger. Perhaps it was Mrs.
Masters.

So few causes for even such a flicker
of curiosity enlivened Arden's days just
now, that she dallied with her impatience.
Then she burst the envelope and read
Mrs. Williams' queer little note, with its
unsuccessful and plebeian elegances.

'How stupid!' was Arden's first ex-
clamation; 'as if I could tell what day
the light would suit me.'

She continued to turn homewards, but
when she got to the gate she hesitated.
What should she do when she reached
home; there were three good hours till
dinner. Her grandfather was ill just
lately, and she might only talk to him
when he had woke up from his after-
dinner nap. Mrs. Lawrance would be
busy and unwilling to have her company.
Should she go on writing letters to the
Roses, letters that were never answered?

or read the back numbers of the 'Gentleman's' all through again ? or half break her back weeding the drive ? It was all very dreary ; yes, much as Arden disliked owning, even to herself, that anything bored her, she must allow that she was supremely weary of the Bushes.

True, she might paint, now she was better. And so she took Mrs. Williams' letter from her pocket, and read it through again. After all it was very good-natured of them to want to see her ; and the orchard was certainly the prettiest subject she had seen. She would go that afternoon.

'At least I can do the blocking in,' she said to herself ; 'and there will be a soul under sixty to talk to.' She walked up the drive, feeling more excited at this prospect of visiting the farmer's sister down the road, than she ever used to be when looking forward to a ball in the old days at Rome.

She forgot that she was tired and disappointed, and instead of going in, she
crossed the farmyard, and walked through
the fields to the farthest field of all, green
now with aftermath. It was a low-lying
lush meadow, sloping down towards the
brook that bordered the farther side ; the
brook itself was hidden under thickly-
sprouting pollard willows, tall reeds and
bulrushes ; and, lower down, mint and
forget-me-not fringed the edges. The
two sides of the field had been so badly
drained, that in damp weather they were
a swamp, and in time of drought an
agglomeration of barren, clayey heaps and
hollows ; the end that joined the little
meadow was partially saved by the roots
of the elms and willows in the hedge ;
but the other side, low and flat, separated
from Farmer Williams's ground by some
railings and a pool, was utterly wasted in
regard to hay or pasture.

But just now it looked so beautiful,
that Arden, at least, would not wish it
otherwise. Among the glaucous tints of
the reeds and flowering rushes, the golden
yellow of the beautiful summer iris had
been dashed and splashed with no niggardly
hand. That corner of the field ; the widening brook edged with silvery willows, the
soft greens and yellows of the sparsely-
grown swamp letting through here and
there a glimpse of the still pool and of the
ripening corn beyond ; that field corner
had struck Arden as a happy subject for a
panel—just a sketch, a mere pochade. So
she stood on the brink of the swamp,
changing her position repeatedly, and the
focus of her eyes, trying to fix in her mind
the outlines of her picture.

Now as it happened Harry Williams
was in the field beyond. She, intent on
her foreground, did not espy him ; but
he, seeing Arden with her wide hat fallen
back like a deep halo round her head and

shoulders, her golden-curled head peeping
just above the golden-flowered irises,
thought her as charming a subject for
study as she thought them. However,
being a very shy and, consciously, an
awkward man, Farmer Williams took good
care that Arden should not be disturbed by
the least sight of an intruder on her loneliness. He kept well behind the hedge
further up the field, and tried to interest
himself in the condition of his crops; but
the memory of Arden's yellow hair made
even the gold of his maturing harvest seem
faded and insufficient.

Probably she might never, or at least
not till long afterwards, have known of his
presence, but for a sudden fancy of hers to
clutch at and carry off some of the lavish
gold of the flowers. For that it was necessary to venture boldly into the heart of the
swamp ; but the topmost clay-ridges were
not yet submerged, and by careful treading

the flowers might be secured at no greater
risk than that of muddy shoes. At first
all went well; but when the spears of the
reeds and flags, the fine stems of the rushes,
and the bold yellow heads of the flowers
were thick all round the girl, shoulder high,
it was less easy to find out a stepping-place;
and if she stood still the soft mud sank to
the water level. At first she laughed,
gathering in her arms a rich harvest of
her spoil. But when her arms were full,
it became no easy problem to get either
backwards or forwards without relinquish-
ing hold of the flowers.

So difficult was it to get backwards
over the quashed and liquid soil, that,
seeing the railings but a few yards ahead,
she determined to venture for them. Once
there it would be easy enough to scramble
along by help of their planks and posts
till she should reach the sudden rise of
the ground. Alas, for her courage! No
sooner had she quitted the yielding sink-

ing ridge on which she stood, than she
floundered hopelessly in the watery mud,
sinking deeper and deeper down among the
reed and lily roots, to the soft miry bottom
where the leeches lurk.

'Santo Dio!' cried Arden, instinctively
stretching out her arms to save herself.
'Oh, my flowers!'

It was dreadful to feel oneself still
going down and not to know where one
would stop, and not to guess how one
would ever extricate oneself—for Arden
was now ankle-deep in the slush. She
saw a man running across the cornfield
towards her.

'Man! Sir! Sentite! O!' And she
shouted a prolonged Italian vocative.

Then she did not cry out any more, for
she saw the man run a little up the field
and return in a moment, still walking very
fast, although bending under the weight of
a broken hurdle which he carried with
him. He crept along the side of the fence,

balancing the hurdle on the top rail, flat, and shoving it along in front of him. Arden, though the mud kept on yielding and yielding, never said a word to hasten him. She looked on fascinated, as though she were the interested watcher at some game of skill. Neither did he speak ; but when, in a moment, he was opposite to her, he stopped. Then he took down the hurdle, set it on one side, and gently lowered it in such a manner that the tall growing reeds and flags were flattened into a sort of mat underneath.

'Now, Miss,' he said.

'But I can't loose my feet!' cried Arden.

'Then you must let me pull you out. I'm 'most afeard, though, th' hurdle will sink under my weight.'

He hesitated for a moment. By this time one foot was free and on the hurdle.

'Oh, I'm safe,' cried Arden. Not yet, though ; for the mud clung close.

'Here, Miss.'

The man had taken off his coat, and he flung it towards her, holding one end.

'Tug at 'n,' he shouted. 'Tug at 'n, I say.'

Another moment and Arden was running over the hurdle—no safe resting-place —towards the railing; yet another, and she was sitting on the safe, dry ground, looking ruefully at her shoes.

' I shall never get home.'

' I'll cut you a swathe of rushes, Miss,' and the man was off again towards the marsh.

He returned, and began binding her feet in the strong clean rushes, and in dragging off this band the black adhering mud was scattered on the grass.

' Oh, don't! don't! ' cried Arden, much more touched by this than even by his more necessary help. 'How can you ? Let me do it myself.'

' Nay, Missie, my red hands are better at this than your white little ones.'

'How kind you are! And I've never thanked you—without you I should still have been sinking, sinking into that horrid bog.'

'Don't mention it, Miss; any man 'ud do as much.'

'But not so cleverly!' cried Arden. 'It was a fine idea to think of the hurdle. I'll never complain of the bad fencing again.'

Harry Williams smiled a sly rustic smile.

''T moight be better!' he said.

'Now it was clever of you,' she went on, 'to turn that defect to such good account. What made you think so suddenly of the hurdle?'

'Well, Miss, you see—the old gentle-man—I beg pardon, Mr. Lawrance,—he's drawing on in years, and he don't see after things as moight be wished. And since the cows were turned into this field—the

fence being so bad they were allus getting
in among the ripening corn.'

'Dear me!' cried Arden, 'what a
shame! I'll tell grandpa!'

Harry Williams took off his hat at this
official declaration, so to speak, of her
identity.

'Nay, Miss Lawrance, don't you trouble.
I was going to say, knowing as th' old
gentleman don't take on much about repairs,
I took the liberty of telling my men to
patch up the railing with planks and
brambles.'

Arden blushed rosy red. It was shameful to let things go to such rack and ruin,
and to trust to the energy of one's neighbours to repair them.

The young man misunderstood her
colouring cheeks.

'I meant no offence, Miss,' he said,
quite earnestly, 'and beg your pardon for
interfering. But see, Miss Lawrance, when

a man's no faddler, no play-farmer, but
sets store by his work, and makes his living
by 't, 'tis a sore worry to have them lump-
ing cows treading down and crushing the
good straight corn.'

'Oh, you mistake!' cried Arden. 'I
was only vexed you should have had the
trouble we ought to have taken.'

'Thank ye, Miss, you're very good.
Well, about th' hurdle. You see the men
had got it out to mend when I heard a cry,
and saw you floundering in the mud with
all yon stinking flags.'

'They're beautiful!' cried Arden.

'Maybe, but yon's their name, and they
don't grow in good pasture.'

'All the same I like them, I call them
yellow lilies ; they grow in Italy.'

'Yes, Miss.'

'But go on, about the hurdle—then you
picked it up and ran to help me.'

'Yes, Miss.'

'And you threw me your coat as a

life-rope.' Arden began to laugh. She suddenly saw the comedy of the situation.

And now it was Harry Williams' turn to blush and look annoyed. With the rustics' awkward, ever-present dread of being ridiculous, all merriment connected with him appeared ill-natured. Luckily Arden went on with her phrase—

'It was like Sir Walter Raleigh and Queen Elizabeth,' she cried. 'It was more than polite, it was courtly.'

Harry, who was not so ignorant as he looked, remembered the tale, and how Raleigh's good fortune and high favour with the Queen were said all to spring from that accidental beginning.

' 'Tis of good omen,' he said.

'No, in the end she was very ungrateful. Now I shall always remember your kindness; and may I ask your name?'

'Williams, Miss.'

'Ah! But of course. How stupid I

was not to see it before. You're the brother of the nice girl who lives in the black-
and-white house ?'

'Yes, Miss Lawrance.'

'You know my name, I see. Will you
thank your mother very much, and say
I'll come to paint the orchard to-morrow
afternoon.'

'Yes, Miss Lawrance. Susie 'll be right
glad.'

'And so shall I; good morning. Thank
you !'

'Good day, Miss.'

She walked off towards the gate.

'How much better he looks in his
working clothes,' she thought. 'It was
really kind of him ; it's very interesting
talking to farmers. One gets to understand the country.'

She had to stay some time unfastening
the broken gate propped up with wood.

'I'm sure the Williams's gates are not
in this condition,' she cried.

And going over the fields homewards, she turned over the whole matter in her mind. 'No,' she said, 'I don't believe Mrs. Lawrance. I am sure he is not a coarse fellow.'

END OF THE FIRST VOLUME.

LONDON: PRINTED BY
SPOTTISWOODE AND CO., NEW STREET SQUARE
AND PARLIAMENT STREET